PUFFIN BOOKS

THE RETURN
OF THE
BAKED BEAN

'That was it! For the rest of my life I would be a Tragic Girl of Mystery wandering the world!'

When Gina Terrific's best friend Rhonda deserts her and her father falls in love, she decides she has to get away.

Swept along in a runaway caravan, Gina finds herself hijacked by a frustrated surfie, Waxhead. She has to think fast to get herself out of some hair-raising and hilarious predicaments in her quest to be a Tragic Girl of Mystery . . .

Following the success of *Me and Barry Terrific*, here is another fast-moving rollicking adventure about Gina and her crazy dad.

By the same author

Me and Barry Terrific

THE RETURN OF THE BAKED BEAN

Debra Oswald

PUFFIN BOOKS

Puffin Books
Penguin Books Australia Ltd
487 Maroondah Highway, PO Box 257
Ringwood, Victoria 3134, Australia
Penguin Books Ltd
Harmondsworth, Middlesex, England
Viking Penguin, A Division of Penguin Books USA Inc.
375 Hudson Street, New York, New York 10014, USA
Penguin Books Canada Limited
2801 John Street, Markham, Ontario, Canada L3R 1B4
Penguin Books (N.Z.) Ltd
182–190 Wairau Road, Auckland 10, New Zealand

First published by Penguin Books Australia, 1990
1 3 5 7 9 10 8 6 4 2
Copyright © Debra Oswald, 1990
Illustrations Copyright © Matthew Martin, 1990

Typeset in 11.5/13pt Times Roman by Syarikat Seng Teik Sdn. Bhd., Malaysia
Made and printed in Australia by Australian Print Group

National Library of Australia
Cataloguing-in-Publication data:

Oswald, Debra.
The return of the baked bean.
ISBN 0 14 034424 1.
1. Title
A823.3

For my nephew, Lucas Oswald Knott

The author would like to thank Richard Glover,
Margaret Connolly, Paul Fisher, Erica Irving, Lisa Jabbour
and the Literature Board of the Australia Council.

For my nephew, Lucas Oswald Knoll

CHAPTER 1

'DON'T act like a raw prawn, Rhonda,' I said, sounding really tough. 'The school bus leaves in five minutes. And we have to be on it.'

Rhonda wailed – making an 'errgghh' choking noise. She curled up on the floor and stuck her long skinny arms and her long skinny legs up in the air. Then she started shaking and jerking her bony arms and legs around: her Dying Cockroach Act.

Rhonda was my Very Best Friend in The Whole World and I have to admit that her Dying Cockroach Act was pretty funny. But there was no way she was going to get out of it. We had to get on that bus.

You see, it was our first day at high school. Year 7 at Muddy Creek High.

'Everyone reckons Muddy Creek High is a really tough place, Gina,' wailed Rhonda. This was true. And I have to admit, we were both pretty terrified. But we didn't have much choice.

'As long as we stick together, we'll be okay,' I said.

The bomby old school bus chugged and coughed and clunked its way up the main street of Borrington, our town. Clouds of black smoke came spewing out the back of it and smelt disgusting.

Rhonda and me climbed on board and looked down the aisle of the bus. It was so noisy you couldn't hear yourself think. The bus was chockablock with kids – all shouting, wrestling, yabbering, throwing stuff, screaming, punching, pinching and spitting. And let me tell you, the inside of that bus smelt revolting. Even at eight o'clock in the morning, it stank of sweat, chewing gum, smelly feet and mud.

'Don't worry,' I whispered back to Rhonda. 'They won't even notice us.'

Unfortunately, I was wrong about that. The next thing we knew there was a shout from the back of the bus.

'Hey, new kids! Little Year 7 wimps!' yelled out a boy up the back.

Every head on the bus turned to look at us. Then they all started yelling – teasing, pointing and laughing, throwing paper darts and generally giving Rhonda and me a hard time. Really childish stuff. I couldn't believe that high school kids could be that juvenile. Apparently they treated all the new Year 7 kids that way.

'Don't let them get to you,' I said. 'I'm an

expert at being a New Kid. I know how to handle it.'

Rhonda nodded nervously. She knew this was true. You see, I went to twenty-eight different primary schools, so I got used to being the New Kid all the time. The reason I went to all those different primary schools was because Barry and me...oh, it gets sort of complicated...

Before I go on with this story, I should explain a couple of things you might not know. You see, for years and years, my dad (Barry Terrific) and me (Gina Terrific) travelled all over Australia selling Dad's amazing inventions and thinking up fabulous schemes to make us famous. None of our schemes ever worked and, in every town we went to, people laughed at Barry for being weird. We had heaps of fun anyway. I didn't mind not having any friends because I had the smartest, funniest, weirdest father in the world. But by the time we got to Borrington, I was sick of always moving around.

In Borrington, I met Rhonda and we became the best friends you could ever imagine. A whole lot of amazing things happened in the town (which you wouldn't believe if I told you) and Dad and me decided to stay put in Borrington from then on.

Now that I've filled you in on that stuff, I can get on with this story properly.

Where was I up to? Oh yeah...well, the bus finally made it to Muddy Creek High and I looked through the scungy window at my new school. There wasn't one tree or one bit of grass anywhere. Just asphalt, concrete, wire fences and ugly buildings with hardly any windows.

'Looks like a prison,' I muttered to Rhonda. Rhonda reckons I have a tendency to exaggerate, but this time she knew I was right. It did look like a prison.

To be really honest, our first day at Muddy Creek High wasn't a great success. It was pretty terrible actually. The Big Kids wouldn't talk to the New Kids and the New Kids were all too scared to talk to anyone. At least Rhonda and me had each other.

We decided to keep a low profile, so we found a little corner beside the drinking bubblers. From there, we could check out how the kids at this school operated.

The school was divided up into lots of different gangs. Rhonda and me counted at least thirty-seven between us. Each gang had a leader and a few other kids who did what the leader told them to do. Everyone was desperate to be in one of the best gangs and they were always swapping and changing.

The leader of the toughest boys was a Year 10 guy called Dwayne Brickman. I reckoned Dwayne looked like a real meathead, but every kid at the school wanted to be mates with him. You should have seen Dwayne cruising round the playground like he owned the place. He really thought he was fantastic. Everyone tried to suck up to Dwayne and only the most popular girls were allowed to hang round with him: Kayleen, Raeleen and Joyleen.

Muddy Creek High had a reputation for being rough and boy, oh, boy, it was true. There was even a *fight* on our first day. Rhonda and me were eating our muesli bars, minding our own business, when we heard these scuffling and grunting noises. In three seconds flat a huge crowd gathered to watch two guys wrestling it out. They cheered and barracked like a crowd at the football or something.

'I reckon it's pathetic,' whispered Rhonda.

'Me too,' I agreed. 'Only meatheads get into fights.'

The trouble was, someone heard me. And that someone happened to be the biggest meathead of all: Dwayne Brickman.

'Whajou say?' said Dwayne Brickman, staring straight at me.

Suddenly, the fight stopped and every kid went quiet. They were all staring at me. I could feel Rhonda's heart pounding beside me, but I played it very cool. That meathead didn't scare me.

'I reckon fighting's dumb. Only meatheads without enough brains have to fight.'

I thought Dwayne Brickman would clobber me for sure. Sometimes my big mouth gets me into lots of trouble. I thought I was a goner. But then a weedy little voice up the back of the crowd piped up.

'Hey, check out the skinny one!' said the weedy kid. He meant Rhonda. He was trying to impress Dwayne by showing how nasty he could be about her.

'She looks like a stick insect!' he sniggered.

It's true that Rhonda was very skinny. In fact, she was the skinniest person I'd ever seen in my life. Sideways she was almost completely flat. If she stood behind a telegraph pole, she disappeared. But I *liked* the way Rhonda looked. I didn't think she looked like a stick insect.

The crowd was silent, waiting to see how Dwayne would react.

'Yeah. Right. A stick insect. Yeah,' said Dwayne and guffawed. Then they all laughed. The whole crowd. Giggling and squealing and cackling until they were blue in the face. The laughter echoed all round the concrete yard, bouncing off the buildings and back at Rhonda even louder.

Poor Rhonda. I could feel her shrivel up beside me. She must have wanted to disappear like an ice-cream melting into the concrete. And you should have seen the mean, dumb smirk on Dwayne Brickman's face. I wanted to thump him on the spot. (I know I said a minute ago that I didn't believe in fighting, but if you'd seen his face you would have agreed with me.) From that

6

day on, every kid in the school (except me of course) called Rhonda 'Stick Insect'.

The thing about a place like Muddy Creek High was that you were either 'in' or 'out'. It was worse-than-dying to be 'out'. (In case you haven't guessed, Rhonda and me were 'out' on account of Rhonda being a Stick Insect.

We got away from that crummy school as soon as we could and raced off to one of our favourite secret places. (I can't tell you where it is because it's the kind of fantastic secret place that would get ruined if too many people knew about it.)

Rhonda wouldn't mind me telling you that she cried that first afternoon after school. You can't blame her really. When a person *needs* to have a good bawling and blubbering session, there's no point saying 'Don't cry'.

When Rhonda calmed down a bit, she tried to be really brave.

'Maybe you should stop being friends with me, Gina,' she sniffed.

'Eh?' I gasped.

'I'm the one who's a Stick Insect. Maybe you could be popular at Muddy Creek High if you dumped me.'

'Rhonda!' I screeched. 'Do you reckon I'd be such a creep? You're my best friend! I wouldn't be friends with those meatheads and nincompoops if you paid me!'

But there was only one way to convince

Rhonda: our Loyalty Oath. You see, last year when Rhonda and me first became friends, we made up a Friendship Loyalty Oath and wrote it out to look like an incredibly old, important scroll. Then we buried it beside the oval outside town.

That afternoon, we dug it up. After a year in the dirt, it looked even more like an ancient parchment.

We read the Oath out loud together: 'We, Gina Terrific and Rhonda Goldwyn, do hereby swear to stay best friends for ever. We promise never to lie to each other or tell stories behind each other's back. We agree never to make fun of anything the other friend wants to do. We must do everything in our power to be the best friends ever. Penalty for breaking this promise is the curse of being bored for ever and ever.'

Because of the crisis, I figured we needed to make the Oath even *more* powerful. So we both pricked our thumbs with a safety-pin and put a spot of blood next to our signatures. You could just *feel* how powerful that Oath was now.

Sticking together. That's how we'd survive Muddy Creek High.

CHAPTER 2

YOU could always tell when Dad was working in his shed (the Invention Workshop). Weird noises, weird smells and puffs of smoke came floating out of our backyard. That's how you'd know that Barry was up to his elbows in some new invention.

All the years we were travelling around the country, Barry and me lived in The Baked Bean. The Bean was a fabulous old caravan (shaped like a baked bean) which Dad had fixed up with heaps of useful inventions and gadgets.

But by the time we decided to live in Borrington, I wanted my own proper bedroom (with walls and a door and everything) and Dad wanted an Invention Workshop. So we found a beaut old wooden house on the edge of town and parked The Baked Bean in the backyard.

The house was pretty crumbly and creaky and Dad was always saying he'd 'fix it up soon'. But I kind of liked it the way it was. It was the first time in my life I had my own room. I set it up to

9

suit me perfectly, with posters on the walls and knick-knacks lined up on the dressing table. I loved my room like crazy.

The Baked Bean was *meant* to be my cubby in the backyard. But cubbies are really only for little kids, so I didn't use it much. The poor old Bean was getting run down – grass grew up round its wheels, paint was flaking off and there was a thick crust of dirt all over it. I felt guilty about neglecting the mighty Bean, but...well...you know...life goes on.

Anyway, when I got home that afternoon, Dad was flat out inventing.

'I'm home!' I yelled out.

'Gina!' came Barry's voice from the shed. 'Home from Day One at high school, eh? I want to hear all about it!'

I headed towards the shed but Dad suddenly poked his head out the door. My dad is one of those people who always seem to look messy, no matter how hard he tries. His curly hair is always sticking out in all directions and clothes never seem to fit properly on his lanky arms and legs. The *best* part about the way Barry looks is his face – he's got the kind of wrinkles around his eyes and mouth that people get from laughing all the time. I would guess that he smiles or laughs about seventy-five percent of the time.

Anyway, that particular afternoon, when Barry stuck his head out the door, he was wearing safety goggles and had a blowtorch in one hand.

'Don't come in yet!' he said, with a big cheesy grin. He was obviously very pleased with himself about something. 'You can't see it yet. We'll go on a test drive!'

'Test drive what?' I asked.

'You'll see. I'll pick you up out the front,' he said and ducked back into the shed.

I sat on the front step and waited. When you grow up with a father like Barry Terrific, you get used to seeing some weird stuff. But even I was surprised by what Dad 'drove' round the corner.

He was driving – and I'm not kidding – an armchair. A big, old, comfortable armchair covered with flowery material. A motorised armchair.

'Two-cylinder, four-on-the-floor,' said Barry proudly. 'I call it the ComfeeCruiser because it's designed for driving round town in maximum comfort. Jump aboard!'

I perched on one arm of the ComfeeCruiser and Dad sat on the seat so he could reach the gearstick. The armchair purred along the road slowly but smoothly. It certainly was very comfortable. Dad and me figured it would be perfect for sick people and old people who still wanted to get around and see stuff. Dad decided he'd make a prototype for Rhonda's grandad to try out.

As we cruised around town in the armchair, people waved or said 'G'day'. People in Borrington had got used to Dad being weird. They weren't at all surprised to see him driving a chair. In fact, most people *liked* having a 'weirdo' in town. They'd point him out to visitors as if he was a tourist attraction.

Dad was raving on about his ideas for the ComfeeCruiser – so excited that his mouth was going at two hundred kilometres an hour. (He's got an amazing brain, my dad.) Barry and me discussed the market potential of the motorised armchair, as we usually did with his inventions.

'I reckon we should celebrate the new invention with a milkshake,' announced Barry.

'A malted milkshake? With extra ice-cream?'

'Of course,' said Dad and parked the Comfee-Cruiser right outside the Borrington milk bar.

We paid for our two caramel malteds (with extra ice-cream) and started slurping up the thick, sweet, gooey, frothy milkshake. I told Barry all about my first day at Muddy Creek High. All about Dwayne Brickman, Rhonda being called a Stick Insect, the ugly buildings – every detail I could remember.

Barry's a fantastic listener. When you're explaining something important, he doesn't butt in with all the usual dumb things people say. You can tell he concentrates on your problem from *your* point of view and then says what he honestly thinks. That's one of the things that makes him such a crackerjack father. (There are about twenty-three other reasons.)

'Hmmm,' said Dad, when I'd finished

explaining. 'It sounds pretty crook, Gina. But you and Rhonda are smart cookies. I bet you'll work something out. At least you've got each other.'

Dad grinned at me, to cheer me up. Even though I still felt lousy, I tried to grin back. I didn't want Barry to worry too much.

We slurped up the last slurps of our milkshakes and headed out to where the ComfeeCruiser was parked. But the ComfeeCruiser was not alone. Standing beside the motorised armchair was a cop – nearly six feet tall, tough, sun-tanned, with huge bulging muscles. The cop was glaring up at Barry and me as though we were in Big Trouble for some reason. She was the new police constable in Borrington.

'Hi there!' said Barry. 'My name's Barry Terrific and this is my daughter Gina. You must be Constable –'

'Constable Brenda Snape,' she said in a snappy voice.

'Welcome! Welcome to Borrington, Constable Snape! It's terrific to –'

'Sir,' interrupted Constable Snape in her snappy voice. 'Is this your vehicle?' She pointed to the ComfeeCruiser.

'It sure is,' said Barry proudly. 'It's a beautie, isn't it?'

'This vehicle is not correctly parked. What does that sign say?'

Barry read the sign out loud. 'Rear to kerb. Forty-five degree angle parking.'

'Exactly,' snapped the new policewoman. 'This armchair is not rear to kerb. I'm going to have to give you a parking ticket.'

Barry laughed, trying to be friendly about it. 'Sure thing, Constable. I understand you're just doing your job. No worries. I mean, where would we be if *everyone* decided to park their armchairs the wrong way round. Hey – how about I take you for a spin in the ComfeeCruiser?'

Constable Snape looked Barry up and down warily. I could tell she was very suspicious about why he was being so friendly. I wanted to warn Dad to play it cool, but there wasn't a chance.

'Don't think you can wriggle out of this parking ticket,' she said in a suspicious voice.

Barry looked confused for a moment and then he looked hurt. He realised Constable Snape thought he was only being nice to get out of paying the fine. She didn't understand that Barry is always friendly to *everyone*. Most people don't understand my dad – he truly likes every person he meets and wants to be helpful. It gets him into trouble sometimes.

'No, no,' Dad grinned, determined to be nice no matter what. 'I'd just like to show you around our beautiful town –'

'Sir,' she interrupted again, 'does this vehicle have indicators or brake lights?'

'Umm – oh – well, no – it doesn't yet,' stammered Barry.

Constable Snape started writing another ticket.

14

While Barry tried to explain about the Comfee-Cruiser being a new invention, the policewoman didn't smile once. She just kept writing out more tickets. She fined Dad for having an unregistered vehicle, an unroadworthy vehicle, driving without a licence, driving without seatbelts. Plus a whole lot of other fines I can't remember.

'I guess you've got to do your job,' said Barry, still trying to be friendly. 'Hey, why don't you stop by our place one evening for some home-made pizza. We'd love to have Constable Snape over since she's new in town, wouldn't we, Gina?'

I tried to signal to Dad to shut up but he couldn't see me. Constable Snape ripped the stack of fines off her police ticket-book and handed them to Barry. He looked at the thick pile of parking tickets in his hand and tried to laugh.

'We haven't got off to a very good start, have we,' he said.

'My advice is to keep this vehicle off the road, Mr Terrific,' barked Constable Snape and marched off.

I watched the new cop striding off down the main street and wondered what would ever make someone like her smile. Dad shook his head and looked kind of sad.

'Brenda Snape. Funny sort of person, eh, Gina.'

CHAPTER 3

THINGS didn't improve for Rhonda and me at Muddy Creek High. In fact, they got worse.

Every day, Rhonda and me sat in our spot near the bubblers and watched the kids at school being really horrible to each other: beating each other up, telling mean stories, snitching on each other, giving Chinese burns, whispering nasty jokes – you name it, they did it. They all thought that Rhonda and me were the biggest jokes of all.

To begin with, it was mostly Rhonda who got teased – for looking like a Stick Insect. But then, at the end of the first week, Rhonda and me were standing in the canteen queue, minding our own business, when a mob of kids headed towards us.

'Oh-oh,' said Rhonda nervously.

'Just ignore them,' I said.

Dwayne Brickman was in front and, as usual, there was a pack of kids following Dwayne around and sucking up to him. Kayleen, Raeleen and Joyleen (the most popular girls in school) kept on giggling and whispering to each other.

'That's the one,' cackled Kayleen. She was pointing straight at me. 'Her.'

'Her father's a real weirdo,' said Raeleen.

'A nut-case. A fruit loop. A loony. A mental-case,' chanted Joyleen.

Dwayne Brickman laughed and all the others joined in. But I didn't care what they thought.

'If her father's a weirdo, that explains how come she's got a Stick Insect for a best friend,' giggled Kayleen.

'Yeah, Gina must be a weirdo mental-case too,' said Raeleen.

'We don't want weirdos in our school,' said Dwayne.

'It might be contagious,' said Joyleen.

I *tried* to ignore them, but finally I'd had enough.

'Get lost,' I snarled.

'Ooh, I'm really scared,' said Dwayne, pretending to shake and look terrified of me.

'You think you're *so* funny, Dwayne Brickman,' I said. 'But in fact you're just incredibly childish. Come on, Rhonda.'

I pulled Rhonda out of the lunch queue and we walked off to the other side of the playground. Behind us, I could hear them all laughing. They called me The Squirt and Stumpy Legs, just because I happen to be the shortest kid in the school. I ignored them. So then they yelled out stupid names like Fuzzy Wuzzy (my curly hair goes a bit frizzy on rainy days), but I kept on

17

ignoring them. You can't let people like that bother you.

No one sat near Rhonda and me in the class-room and no one wanted to be in our team for basketball. There was no way any of the other kids would be friends with us. Because if they did, they'd get teased too.

'Just remember our Friendship Loyalty Oath,' I said to Rhonda. 'It doesn't matter how mean those kids are, if we stick together. We're still the best friends in the whole world.'

Rhonda nodded, but you could tell it bothered her more than me. I caught her staring at Kayleen, Raeleen and Joyleen on the other side of the playground where they were giggling with Dwayne.

'I wonder what it'd be like to be really popular like Kayleen, Raeleen and Joyleen,' she said with a sad little sigh.

The next Saturday afternoon, Dad, Rhonda and me were leaning up against the counter of the Borrington milk bar, just hanging around the way we liked to do sometimes. In the street in front of us was a weird and wonderful sight.

You see, word had got around town about the ComfeeCruiser motorised armchair and *all* the old folks in Borrington wanted their own. So Dad had been working day and night manufacturing more ComfeeCruisers.

Now the main street of town was full of Senior

18

Citizens chugging up and down in motorised armchairs – going visiting, doing their shopping or taking in the sights.

'Y'know, Mr Terrific,' said Rhonda, 'I reckon the ComfeeCruiser is one of your best inventions ever.'

'Thank you, Rhonda. You are most kind,' said Dad in a really posh voice and bowed to Rhonda like a prince or someone. You could tell Dad was really enjoying himself. If other people were happy, he was happy. There was only *one* problem. A big problem which appeared in the doorway of the Borrington milk bar. Constable Brenda Snape.

'G'day, Constable Snape,' said Dad chirpily, *still* trying to be friendly. 'How's it all going for you? Crackerjack day, eh?'

'Mr Terrific,' Constable Snape said, without smiling one tiny bit, 'these vehicles of yours are causing a major traffic hazard in this town.'

'Oh...I'm sorry...maybe we can –'

'I think you'd better come down to the police station first thing Monday morning to discuss the situation,' she snapped. And without even saying goodbye, she twisted round on her heel and crunched her shiny black boots out of the milk bar.

Constable Snape never left Dad alone. She was always checking up on him and always giving him a hard time about something or other. 'Do you have safety clearances for these contraptions, Mr

Terrific?' 'Do you have a licence to manufacture, Mr Terrific?' 'Have you filled out form 24B, Mr Terrific?' and so on and so on.

Constable Snape made Dad pay fines for breaking fire regulations, traffic regulations, council ordinances, safety rules, licensing laws, and heaps more. She must have given him *twenty* parking tickets. No one else in town ever got parking tickets for parking in the same places we did. Constable Snape didn't even bother to fine any of the old folks chugging around on Comfee-Cruisers. She just bothered Dad.

To begin with, Dad tried to be understanding. 'Constable Snape is just doing her job,' he'd say. When the fines arrived in the post, he made excuses for her: 'Constable Snape works very hard', 'Maybe Constable Snape isn't a very happy person'. But eventually even Dad got sick of it. All he wanted to do was to create inventions to help people out. This narky cop was making it difficult.

After Constable Snape's blue uniform disappeared round the corner of the milk bar, Dad didn't say anything for a minute or two. His face was creased up with worry and he was grinding his teeth together a little bit.

'Y'know, girls,' he said finally, in a funny quiet voice, 'I like just about everyone I meet. I reckon there's always *something* to like about a person. But Constable Snape...I don't know, Gina and Rhonda. I've tried to be friendly. I've tried to do the right thing. I've tried to like that policewoman. But I've got to admit, I don't think I like Constable Brenda Snape.'

I looked at Rhonda. Rhonda looked at me. Both of us had our mouths hanging open. I'd never in my whole life heard Dad say that about *anyone*.

You could tell Barry felt pretty bad about it, so Rhonda and me didn't make a fuss. Rhonda ordered another round of milkshakes to take his mind off it.

An old bloke chugged past the milk bar on a ComfeeCruiser and made a 'thumbs up' gesture to Dad.

'What a little beautie!' called out the old bloke. Barry made an 'okay' signal back and his sad face cracked into a smile. It didn't take long for Dad to start cracking jokes again. Barry doesn't believe in feeling sorry for yourself.

'You heading down to the rodeo tomorrow, Barry?' croaked the old bloke.

'I don't know anything about a rodeo,' Barry yelled back.

'Aww, ya should get down there and have a look. The Burragoranga Annual Rodeo. One of the big events of the year!'

'Thanks for the tip, mate,' Dad grinned, as the old bloke chugged off into the distance.

'What do you reckon, girls?' asked Dad. 'There's no point me moping about that policewoman and there's no point you two moping about Muddy Creek High. Let's go to the rodeo!'

CHAPTER 4

BURRAGORANGA was *buzzing*. Even three kilometres away, Dad and Rhonda and me could see a giant cloud of dust hanging over the town. The dust was kicked up from the wheels of all the buses and trucks and utilities that were roaring into Burragoranga. People poured in from all over the district and from all over Australia for the Burragoranga Annual Rodeo. More than ten thousand people turned up and, believe me, in a small town like Burragoranga, that's a *lot* of people.

The showground carpark was chockablock with rows of huge shiny interstate coaches, and out of the coaches poured hundreds of people busting to see the rodeo. Rodeo fans drove down all the way from Queensland for the weekend. There was even a helicopter that buzzed in and landed on the front lawn of the town hall to drop off some rich bloke from Sydney.

Dad, Rhonda and me leaned ourselves up

against the front of the Burragoranga 'Paragon' milk bar to watch the action. Cars could hardly crawl up the main street because of the swarms of people. There was a kind of sea of Akubra stockmen's hats bobbing along in front of us. Cowboy boots crunched and clumped up and down the street. Horses clopped along the gutters and footpaths, ridden by cowboys and cowgirls wearing flashy rodeo outfits.

Country and Western music seemed to be playing everywhere – blasting out of car radios and pouring out of shop doorways, until every nook and cranny of the street was filled up with the sound. The three of us couldn't resist tapping our feet to the twanging and thumping music all around us.

Everyone seemed so friendly. Whenever Barry smiled at someone going past, they'd smile back and say 'G'day' – tilting their hats back a bit and nodding in the way that blokes from the bush always do.

'You know what we need to get into the swing of things, you guys?' said Dad.

'What?' I asked.

'Hats!'

And straight away, he dived into a store and bought us an Akubra hat each. As soon as we got outside, we threw our new hats in the dirt and scuffed them up a bit with our shoes. To look absolutely *right*, our hats had to look as old and beaten-up as the hats on the heads of the real bushies. Walking up the main street in our new dusty hats, we felt pretty cool, I can tell you.

'Glad we came, mate?' asked Barry.

'You bet,' I said and I meant it.

'It's great, Mr Terrific. Thanks a lot,' said Rhonda.

I thumped Rhonda in the ribs with my elbow. She always broke me up when she said stuff like that. She's such a polite person.

'I bet you girls have forgotten about Muddy Creek High already,' said Dad.

He was right. I was so busy gawking and rubbernecking at the rodeo, I actually forgot about Dwayne Brickman, Kayleen, Raeleen and Joyleen and all those creeps for a while. And I reckon Dad forgot about his troubles with Constable Snape too.

No matter how bad things got at Muddy Creek High, I figured I was one of the luckiest people in the world. There I was at this crackerjack rodeo, with an Akubra hat on my head, with the best father and the best friend in the world.

Little did I know that something TERRIBLE was about to happen, followed by something even more TERRIBLE to ruin my whole life.

When the main rodeo events were about to start, huge swarms of people headed up the road to the town's sportsground. The rodeo arena was set up in the middle with big banks of seats all around it for the spectators. Dad, Rhonda and me hurried to catch up with the crowds, so we could get a good seat up the front.

Closer to the main arena, the smell of horses, cattle, manure and straw got stronger and thicker.

'Don't you just love that smell?' I said to Rhonda.

'Yeah,' she said, sniffing deeply. 'It's even better if you close your eyes.'

As usual, Rhonda was right. We both stopped for a second, closed our eyes and took a deep breath in.

When we opened our eyes again, Dad had disappeared.

'Over here, Gina!' he yelled. Barry was waving to us from a stall marked 'Event Entries'.

'Uh-oh,' I said to Rhonda. 'I hope Dad isn't thinking about entering any of the rodeo events.'

Dad was as revved up as a little kid at Luna Park. 'I've decided to enter a couple of these rodeo events, Gina!'

'But Dad –' I began.

'It won't be dangerous, Gina. Don't you worry. I'm only going in the ones that aren't dangerous.'

'But Dad –' I tried again.

'I can't just sit on my bum and watch everyone else having all the fun!' Dad said. 'You've gotta get in there and have a go at things!' (My dad is a big believer in 'Getting in there and having a go at things'.)

'Don't do anything silly, Dad,' I yelled out,

wagging my finger like a cranky old school-teacher. 'Promise you'll be careful.'

'Cross my heart and hope to die,' Dad promised. And he ducked away, disappearing into the crowd along with all the other Akubra hats, before I had a chance to argue.

Rhonda and me squeezed into a spot on a front bench with a perfect view of the arena. I have to admit I was pretty nervous. My Dad gets so carried away and enthusiastic sometimes, that he doesn't realise how dangerous things can be. Usually, I manage to keep him out of trouble. But not this time.

As usual, Rhonda knew exactly what I was thinking. Sometimes, it was *spooky* the way she understood what went on in my head.

'Don't worry about Barry,' said Rhonda. 'He'll be right.'

'What if he really hurts himself?' I said nervously.

'Look, Gina, you know there's no way you could've talked him out of it,' Rhonda pointed out. 'Once Barry gets an idea in his head, he can be as stubborn as you are.' (She understands my dad almost as well as I do.)

It was too late anyway. There was a crackle of sound over the loudspeaker.

'Can I have your attention, ladies and gentlemen,' said the loudspeaker. 'Welcome to the twenty-third Annual Burragoranga Championship Rodeo. The first event on today's programme is Bronco Riding, Open Division. The first contestant is B.Terrific from Borrington, New South Wales.'

There was my dad sitting on top of a bucking bronco in the horse-yard, grinning at me like a little kid on a merry-go-round.

The idea of the Bronco Riding event was to try and stay on the horse for as long as possible while it bucked and jumped around. Even the really good championship riders only lasted a little while before they got tossed off.

Well, to be really honest, my dad didn't last very long on the horse. In fact, if you blinked your eyes, you'd have missed him completely.

As soon as the horse-yard gate was opened, Barry's horse burst out into the arena with Barry on its back. But Dad only lasted half a second. The horse bucked up its rear legs and Dad went flying off into the air. He hit the dust with a thud.

That thud was the worst sound I'd ever heard. I flinched, feeling the thud in my bones, as if it was me who'd hit the ground. All through the arena, there was an 'ooh-aah' sound from the crowd. Spectators leaned forward, worried whether Dad was all right.

At exactly the same moment, Rhonda and me jumped over the barrier and hurtled straight across the arena to where Barry lay in the dirt.

'Dad! Dad, are you okay?'

Dad didn't seem to be moving at all. He just lay there in a little cloud of dust with his new

Akubra hat flopped over his face. As I kneeled down in the dirt beside him, I was so worried, I thought I was going to be sick.

'Gina – I think I saw his hand move!' gasped Rhonda, bug-eyed with worry.

Slowly, very slowly, Dad's hand lifted up and pushed the hat back from his face, just like a real bloke from the bush.

'No worries, Gina,' he croaked, panting for air. 'I'm okay, mate.'

I nearly fainted with relief – truly. Behind me, I could hear the crowd moan an 'aahh' of relief too.

Suddenly there was a pair of boots beside Dad's head. Black, knee-high, cowboy boots with fancy designs carved in the leather and curly silver toecaps.

I didn't know who was wearing those fabulous boots and Dad didn't either. My eyes followed the boots up to see who was in them. The boots belonged to a woman wearing the most fantastic outfit I'd ever seen. A razza-matazz rodeo outfit made out of spangly white material and covered in red tassels. To finish off the spectacular outfit was a white ten-gallon hat with a sparkly red band around it.

The sun dazzled and glinted on the red tassels and white spangles as the rodeo woman looked down at Dad and me on the ground. From where we were in the dust, half-blinded by the sun, she looked like something out of a dream – some fabulous glittering vision. She put out her hand to help Dad up. It was only then that I realised who she was.

'That was a bit of a nasty fall, Mr Terrific,' said Constable Brenda Snape. 'Can I give you a hand up?'

Cross my heart and hope to die, it truly was Constable Snape. And she was giving Dad the biggest, flashiest grin I'd ever seen. Dad blinked a couple of times and shook his head. He thought he must be seeing things.

Constable Snape grinned again. 'If you don't hop out of the way, you're likely to get trampled on, Mr Terrific,' she said with a little laugh.

Like a zombie, Dad took her hand and let himself be hauled up and led out of the rodeo arena. The next thing we knew, the rodeo woman had disappeared. Like some comic-book superhero. Maybe we had imagined the whole thing.

CHAPTER 5

'WHO was that woman?' Dad gasped, with his eyes wide and glassy as if he'd seen a ghost.

An old bushie sitting next to us chuckled. 'Don't you know who she is? That was Brenda Snape! She just happens to be one of the greatest Australian rodeo stars of all time! All-Round Women's Champion five years running.'

'It just shows you,' said Rhonda, shaking her head, 'that you never can tell about a person.'

For the rest of the day, Dad couldn't take his eyes off Brenda Snape. Whenever she came into the arena on her gorgeous glossy black horse Zorro, the crowd went wild – cheering and clapping. And you could see why. She was fantastic, brilliant, incredible.

You should have seen Brenda and Zorro working together. It was as though she and the horse could read each other's minds. (A bit like Rhonda and me, I suppose.) Constable Snape hardly had to twitch and Zorro would do exactly what she wanted him to do. Together, they darted and danced around that rodeo arena – the perfect team. They made it all look incredibly easy, even though you knew it wasn't easy at all.

None of the other rodeo riders had a chance of winning against them. Brenda and Zorro won every event they competed in – the Breakaway Roping, the Barrel Racing, the Calf Roping and lots more.

Rhonda and me couldn't stop raving about Constable Snape.

'Isn't she incredible!' gushed Rhonda.

'Aww yeah!' I gushed back.

'Wouldn't you just *die* to be able to ride like that!'

'And have a horse like Zorro!'

'Aww yeah!' Rhonda gasped. 'I'd just *die* to have a horse like Zorro!'

Whenever Constable Snape finished an event, she'd whip off her spangly red and white hat and wave it above her head, flashing a huge smile to the crowd. Zorro would rear up his front legs and then bow right down, stretching out one front leg and curling the other one back. You could tell Zorro loved being a show-off for the audience. The crowd went crazy – whooping and whistling and clapping till their hands were red-raw.

Rhonda and me clapped and whooped and whistled as loudly as everyone else. (Rhonda can do a pretty impressive whistle when she puts her mind to it.) But the weird thing was that Barry didn't cheer or clap or say one word. Normally, my dad is the most enthusiastic person you could meet. Normally, he yells out 'Bravo!' when someone is good, let alone as fabulous as Constable Snape and Zorro.

But Barry did not make one sound. He just sat there like a zombie, never taking his eyes off Constable Snape.

'Hey, Gina,' whispered Rhonda, 'what's up with your dad?'

'I dunno,' I shrugged. 'Maybe he's still feeling funny after his fall.'

When the last event was over and Brenda Snape was announced as the All-Round Women's Champion, the crowd cheered and stamped themselves into a frenzy. In two seconds flat, Constable Snape was swamped by a mob of people wanting her autograph.

'Maybe if we hurry, we can get an autograph too,' said Rhonda.

But when we got up to go, Dad didn't move. He was frozen to the seat, staring across the arena at Constable Snape with huge, wild eyes. Rhonda pulled a 'What's up with him?' face and I pulled an 'I don't have a clue' face.

'Are you okay, Dad?' I asked.

Barry didn't really answer me. He was talking to himself out loud, I reckon.

'What a woman...' he murmured.

'What did he say?' Rhonda nudged me with her bony elbow.

'I think he's talking about Constable Snape,' I said.

In fact, Constable Snape was all Barry could talk about now. He just kept murmuring 'What a woman' and shaking his head like he couldn't believe it.

'Did you see her, Gina? Did you see Constable Snape?' he gasped.

'Of course I did. I was sitting right next to you, Dad.'

'Wasn't she fabulous! I've never met a woman like that! I can't believe it's the same person! I've never seen anyone so – so…I've never met anyone with such – such…Brenda Snape! What a women…she's – she's she's…' It was the first time in my life I'd ever seen my dad at a loss for words.

'Would you like us to get her autograph for you, Mr Terrific?' Rhonda offered.

'Yes. Yes, thank you, Rhonda. I'd like that very much.'

I was really worried now. I'd never seen my dad acting like this. I opened my mouth to say something, but Rhonda grabbed my arm and dragged me off to join the autograph queue.

When we finally got to the head of the queue, Constable Snape was very friendly in a shy kind of way. She signed our rodeo programmes and then said, 'Is your father okay?'

'Yep,' I said.

'Except that he's acting like a zombie,' said Rhonda. Boy, can that girl be a big-mouth sometimes. I thumped her in the ribs secretly to tell her to shut up about Dad.

'There's a barbeque and campfire singalong tonight if you and your father would like to stay around for it,' said Brenda Snape.

'Aww, beautie!' blurted Rhonda, the big-mouth. 'We'd love that, wouldn't we, Gina!'

I just shrugged. I wasn't so sure. Barry was acting so strangely that I was getting a weird feeling about this whole rodeo business.

It was one of those dead-clear nights when the sky is a thick spongy black, chockablock with stars. Next to the cattle-yards and rodeo arena, an enormous campfire was thrumming and crackling. Rhonda and me sat on a pile of feedsacks, watching the sparks from the fire shooting up and then disappearing against the black sky.

The orangey firelight flickered on to the spangles of Brenda Snape's rodeo outfit, making it look even more fabulous and glamorous. Rhonda nudged me and pointed to Dad, sitting on a tree-stump next to us. He hadn't eaten one mouthful of dinner. He was just staring at Brenda Snape.

'I reckon,' whispered Rhonda, 'that Barry has the hots for her.'

'My dad?' I said. 'No way.'

'Wanna bet?' said Rhonda. 'I bet you a malted

milkshake every day for a week that your dad has the hots for Brenda Snape.'

'You're on,' I said.

'Hey, Mr Terrific – have you got the hots for Constable Snape?' Rhonda asked matter-of-factly. (Rhonda doesn't believe in beating around the bush.)

'You know what – I think I do,' said Dad.

'I thought so,' said Rhonda, shovelling in another mouthful of coleslaw. 'I've seen it on TV. Why don't you go and tell her?'

I nudged Rhonda in the ribs to make her shut up but it was too late. Dad had made up his mind. He got straight up and marched past the campfire to where Constable Snape was standing.

'Excuse me. I just wanted to say that I think you're fantastic and I think I'm in love with you,' he blurted out in one go.

The way Brenda Snape had always acted to Barry, you might have expected her to thump him on the spot. But she didn't.

She melted into Dad's arms – just like the big lovey-dovey kiss at the end of a movie.

I was wrong. Rhonda was right. My dad and Constable Snape were madly in love. It turned out that Constable Snape had fallen in love with Barry the very first day she'd seen him on the ComfeeCruiser. But, being a shy sort of person, she didn't know what to say. Because she wasn't very good with words, Constable Snape had tried

to express her love with parking tickets. She'd
hounded Dad with fines and stuff so she could go
on seeing him every day. But Dad had never got
the message.

I thought it was the stupidest thing I'd ever
heard, but Rhonda reckoned that she'd read
about that sort of thing in a magazine. Rhonda
reckoned it was like the boy at school who
punches you hardest because he loves you the
most. Pretty dumb, if you ask me.

Well, now that Barry and Constable Snape had
admitted they loved each other, they wanted to
be together *all the time*. At the police station, at
the milk bar, at our place, in Dad's Invention
Workshop, you name it. They'd go for long walks
down at the creek with Brenda's gorgeous black
horse Zorro following along behind like a puppy.
Dad and Constable Snape were always together.

And when they were together, they were so
mushy. Always raving on with lots of lovey-
dovey stuff. It was enough to make a person sick.

I hardly saw my dad any more, because he was
always off somewhere with Constable Snape. I
have to admit I was a teeny weeny bit jealous. I
mean, Dad and me used to be best mates but now
that policewoman was always hanging around. I
didn't even like her much.

'How come you don't like her anyway?' said
Rhonda, who thought Brenda Snape was good
value. 'You thought she was fabulous at the
rodeo.'

'Aww...that was before,' I mumbled sulkily.

'Anyway,' said Rhonda, 'I reckon you should be glad your dad is in love with someone who loves him back.'

Rhonda was right, I suppose. Actually, I think Rhonda is a very wise person sometimes. I decided I shouldn't mind too much about Dad and Constable Snape because I had Rhonda. Now that Barry was always off somewhere with the policewoman, Rhonda and me spent even more time together. In fact, apart from when we were actually *asleep*, you could say that Rhonda and me were always together.

Muddy Creek High was still the Worst School In The Whole World and the kids there still treated Rhonda and me like dirt. But we were even better best friends than ever before, so we could survive anything.

But little did I know that the next TERRIBLE thing was about to happen which would ruin my whole life.

CHAPTER 6

A FLASH red sports car – one of those shiny, flattened-out type of cars – was parked outside the Muddy Creek High School gate. Dwayne Brickman eavesdropped through the headmaster's office door. And that was how the rumour got started. The rumour spread round Muddy Creek High like a bad smell. Apparently some people from the city were going to make a TV commercial at our school.

At lunchtime, the headmaster made us all line up in the assembly hall. All the kids were wriggling and squirming and chattering about the TV people and what was going to happen. Rhonda and me stood close together in the back corner, playing it cool.

'Settle down, settle down,' said the headmaster, waving his hands up and down to make everyone shut up. 'I'd like to introduce Miss Vanessa Stapleton-Jones.'

Miss Vanessa Stapleton-Jones stood beside him on the podium, oozing this sickly sweet smile at all of us kids. She was as flash as her flash car and as fancy as her fancy name, dolled up in glamorous clothes like a model, and with so much make-up caked on her face that you couldn't see her skin any more.

'Miss Stapleton-Jones is from Big-Shot Productions and they want to make a television commercial at Muddy Creek High.'

Big deal. We already knew that.

'Miss Stapleton-Jones would also like to see if there is a student at this school who would be suitable to appear in the television advertisement.'

One of us kids was going to get to *be in* the TV ad! All through the assembly hall there were squeals of excitement and a flutter of whispers.

'Settle down,' said the headmaster, flapping his arms.

We had to stand still in rows while Miss Stapleton-Jones walked up and down. Close behind her was another city bloke, carrying one of those instant cameras. The way the TV lady looked each kid up and down, it felt like we were prize cattle on show. But no one seemed to care. Every single kid in that assembly hall was *busting* to be picked out.

As she walked along the rows, a little cloud of perfume wafted behind her. She must have poured a bucket of perfume all over herself. The sickly sweet smell clogged up my nose and made me feel queasy in the tummy.

When she got to Rebecca Moss (a girl in Year 9), Miss Stapleton-Jones stopped and flashed one of her sickly sweet smiles. She asked Rebecca's name and some other stuff which she scribbled in a notebook. She got the bloke with the camera to take a photo of Rebecca giving a cheesy grin.

When the TV people moved further along the row, Rebecca and her friends collapsed into a giggling heap. I guess they thought Rebecca was going to be picked for the ad.

But the TV lady wrote down a few more names and took a few more photos. So we couldn't tell who would be picked.

'Psst, Gina,' whispered Rhonda, nudging me with her bony elbow. 'I bet she picks Kayleen, Raeleen or Joyleen. Wanna bet?'

But Miss Stapleton-Jones walked straight past the three most popular girls in the school. Kayleen's mouth was hanging open like she couldn't believe she wasn't picked. Raeleen and Joyleen just pouted sulkily.

'I feel like an idiot standing here,' said Rhonda. 'There's no way she'll pick either of us.'

'No way,' I agreed.

As the lady got closer, the cloud of perfume got thicker. I felt a tickle in my nose. I tried to control it but I just couldn't help a huge sneeze exploding out.

Miss Stapleton-Jones looked up from her notebook at me, as I recovered from the monster sneeze. Then she looked sideways at Rhonda.

Her eyes went very wide and a little squeak of surprise came out of her lipstick-covered mouth.

'Perfect!' she gasped. 'Absolutely perfect!'

'Sorry?' said Rhonda.

'You're perfect for the commercial!' gushed Miss Stapleton-Jones, squeezing Rhonda's arm with her bright red fingernails.

'Me?' said Rhonda, flabbergasted.

'Her?' said Kayleen, who couldn't believe it either.

'The Stick Insect?' said Dwayne Brickman.

Every kid in the school was gawking at Rhonda. Why would they want someone who looked like Rhonda on TV? It must've been a mistake.

But it wasn't a mistake. Miss Stapleton-Jones hooked her arm round Rhonda and whisked her straight out of the assembly hall.

Rhonda reckoned they took about a hundred photos of her and then whizzed her home in the red sports car. Rhonda's mum had to sign the forms to say Rhonda could be in the ad. Apparently, they *wanted* someone skinny and unusual – just like Rhonda in fact. You can never tell what those flash city people will want.

Anyway, the next day, Miss Stapleton-Jones's red sports car and three huge trucks full of film equipment were parked outside Muddy Creek High. Rhonda got the day off school so she could be in the ad. And the rest of us were allowed out early so we could watch the filming.

41

The corner of the playground near the canteen was chockablock with cameras, lights, electric cables and other film junk. And heaps of people! I couldn't believe it took that many people to make one little commercial.

In the middle of all that fuss was my best friend Rhonda, looking as calm and cool as anything. That's the sort of person Rhonda is. She doesn't get into a tizz about things.

It was an ad for Mrs Richard's Country Muffins. Rhonda was meant to be this wiry, cheeky country kid who buys one of the muffins at the canteen. She had to eat the muffin like it was the most delicious thing she'd eaten in her whole life and then skip off across the yard.

Every kid in the school was jammed together behind a little barricade so we wouldn't get in the way of the filming. Everyone was busting to see how a commercial was made. I could see Kayleen, Raeleen and Joyleen talking to Dwayne Brickman. They all looked pretty sulky to me. Kayleen was whispering to Dwayne and pointing at Rhonda. I bet they were feeling pretty stupid on account of being nasty to Rhonda the TV star.

I know it sounds mean, but I was feeling *so* glad that Rhonda got picked instead of them. Dad reckons you should never gloat. But you've got to admit, sometimes gloating is fun.

From what I could see, the ad people made Rhonda do everything about twenty times. Over and over again. I couldn't see why. Rhonda had to take a bite of the muffin and make a face about how great it tasted. The director of the ad yelled out, 'Terrific, sweetheart. That was perfect.' But then he made her do it again and again. It didn't make much sense to me. Rhonda ended up eating enough muffins to make a person sick.

Rhonda told me afterwards that the muffins were disgusting – all claggy inside and tasting of cardboard. But if you'd seen Rhonda eating the muffin for the ad, you'd swear she *loved* them. That just shows you what a good actress Rhonda is.

When it was all over, the ad director gave Rhonda a hug and a big sloppy kiss, raving on about how terrific she was. Even Miss Stapleton-Jones gave Rhonda a peck on both cheeks.

Rhonda strolled away from the cameras, across the yard, towards the barricades. The crowd of kids parted to make way for her. They were all incredibly impressed, you could tell. Rhonda acted very suave – she's such a drama-puss – and just winked at me on the sly.

'I thought you were terrific, Rhonda,' I said. 'I reckon you could be a famous actress if you wanted.' I was *so* proud of Rhonda that day.

You see, Rhonda starring in the TV ad wasn't the SOMETHING TERRIBLE. The TERRIBLE part happened next.

CHAPTER 7

ALL of a sudden, Rhonda was popular. In fact, one of the most popular kids at Muddy Creek High. As soon as the filming was over, Kayleen, Raeleen and Joyleen started sucking up to her.

'Hi, Rhonda,' said Kayleen, sounding really smarmy. 'We thought you were great in the TV ad.'

'Oh...umm...thank you,' mumbled Rhonda, not quite sure how to react.

'What was it like being in an ad?' asked Raeleen.

'Yeah, Rhonda, tell us everything the TV people said to you,' said Joyleen, as nice as pie all of a sudden. The three most popular girls in the school surrounded Rhonda, asking lots of questions, flattering her and generally sucking up. Rhonda sneaked a look at me and pulled a face as if to say 'What's going on?'

That was only the beginning. The next day, every kid at that lousy school wanted to be Rhonda's friend.

'I don't get it, Gina,' said Rhonda, screwing up her face, baffled. 'How come everyone's being so nice to me all of a sudden?'

'It's obvious, dummy,' I said. I couldn't believe Rhonda was being so thick. 'Because they all want to be mates with the star of a TV commercial.'

Lots of kids asked Rhonda if she'd like to sit with them at lunchtime. But Rhonda just said 'No thanks, I'm sitting with Gina.' She knew we were best friends. Or at least, I *thought* she knew.

So Rhonda and me sat in our usual spot beside the bubblers, eating lunch the way we always did. (I swapped one of my cheese and Vegemite sandwiches for one of Rhonda's tuna ones.) But things were different now. Kids kept smiling and saying 'Hi' to Rhonda. You could see Rhonda was sort of enjoying all the attention. At least no one was calling her Stick Insect any more. I think it went to her head a little bit.

You see, all her life, Rhonda was always an outsider, always an odd girl out. Like me. Neither of us ever had a friend until we met each other. Anyway, the point is, Rhonda really enjoyed being popular for once. She liked having lots of friends. You can't blame her for that. I'm not trying to make excuses for Rhonda. I'm just trying to *explain* what happened.

'You know, Gina,' said Rhonda thoughtfully, 'Kayleen, Raeleen and Joyleen are quite nice once you get to know them.'

'You reckon? Blaagghh!' I said. I didn't like those three girls *at all*.

'They're nicer than we thought they were,' she went on. 'Maybe we should be friends with them.'

'Oh...maybe...' I mumbled. I sounded very sulky, I have to admit. Those popular girls didn't want to be friends with *me*. Just with Rhonda, the TV star. Rhonda could tell I was sulking. It's amazing how she always knows what I'm thinking.

'Don't worry, Gina,' she said. 'You and me will still be best friends. For ever.'

I nodded. I *thought* Rhonda meant what she said.

But then, believe it or not, Dwayne Brickman – the toughest kid in the whole school – waved to Rhonda across the playground.

'Hey, Rhonda,' yelled out Dwayne Brickman, oh-so-friendly. 'Why don't you come over here for a second.'

Rhonda looked at me, completely amazed that Dwayne Brickman would want to talk to her. 'What should we do?' she whispered.

I could tell Rhonda really *wanted* to go over there. So we got up and started walking across towards Dwayne Brickman and his mates. But halfway across the yard, Dwayne yelled out: 'Just you, Rhonda. Not Gina.'

Rhonda hesitated. I shrank back a few steps. So now Rhonda was stuck in the middle – halfway between me and the popular kids. You could tell from her face she was confused. She didn't know which way to go. More than anything else in the whole world, I wanted her to turn around, to forget about those popular kids and be my friend.

But she didn't.

'I'll just talk to Dwayne for a minute, Gina,' she said and skipped off towards the other kids.

I felt like someone had slugged me in the guts. If someone had told me Rhonda would do that, I *never* would have believed it.

'Psst, Gina,' Kayleen whispered in my ear like a snake. 'We all reckon Rhonda should dump you. Now that she's going to be friends with us, she can't be friends with you any more.'

Maybe it was true. I knew Kayleen was trying to be mean, but I couldn't help panicking. Maybe Rhonda *would* dump me. Just then, I heard Rhonda's barking laugh. I always loved the weird way Rhonda laughed. I looked up to see that Dwayne Brickman was telling Rhonda a joke. Rhonda and Dwayne were getting on like a house on fire. Rhonda had forgotten all about me. I felt sick. I was about to burst into tears. But there was no way I was going to let any of those creeps see me crying.

Tears were burning on my eyeballs as I scuttled out of the playground. I couldn't hold back from howling much longer. Not without every kid in the playground seeing me.

I managed to scramble into one of the empty classrooms before I dissolved into tears. I couldn't face going out into the playground again. I decided to hide out in the empty classroom until lunchtime was over.

Maybe by the end of lunchtime, Rhonda would come to her senses. She'd realise that I was her best friend and that she shouldn't hang around with those popular creeps. Yep, I was sure that in no time at all, Rhonda and me would be back together again.

The bell went for the end of lunchtime. The sound of running feet thundered up and down the concrete corridors as all the kids hurried to class.

I sat in the middle of the front row, where Rhonda and me always sat. (The popular kids got to sit in the back row which was the coolest place to sit.)

Kids started to clatter into the classroom and saw me sitting on my own. I heard a couple of them snigger.

'Hey!' bellowed some boofhead kid. 'Who wants to sit next to Weird Gina?'

All through the classroom, there was a roar of laughter, insults and nasty jokes. I couldn't wait for Rhonda to arrive and come and sit in her spot right beside me. Then I wouldn't care what any of those creeps said about me.

Just at that second, Rhonda came through the classroom door surrounded by smarmy popular kids. She could see what was going on. She could see that they were giving me a hard time. She *knew* that wasn't fair. But Rhonda also knew that, if she said so, she'd be in trouble.

Rhonda looked at me and then at her new friends sniggering and pointing at me. She looked at the seat beside me in the front row where she had always sat. She had to choose. She could stay with her new friends and be a popular girl at school. Or she could stick up for me and wreck her chances of ever being popular again.

Rhonda's face went all crinkled up with worry. I knew exactly what she was thinking (on account of us understanding each other so well). Her new friends tugged at Rhonda's sleeve.

'C'mon, Rhonda,' one of them said. 'Let's go up the back. We don't want to sit at the front near *her*.'

And – believe it or not – Rhonda went. She went down to the back row with the popular kids and left me stranded on my own. I couldn't believe it. Rhonda Goldwyn turned her back on her best friend. Rhonda Goldwyn wimped out completely.

That was the final slug in the guts for me. I'd *never* forgive Rhonda for not sticking up for me. Never in a million years. At that moment, I made a vow to myself.

'I swear,' I whispered to myself so no one would overhear, 'that I will never forgive Rhonda Goldwyn and never speak to her ever again for a million years.'

The rest of the afternoon at Muddy Creek High was probably the worst afternoon of my entire life. In front of the other kids, I acted like I didn't need a best friend any more. I pretended I was happier on my own. This was a huge fib, of course. Without Rhonda, Muddy Creek High was the loneliest place on the entire earth, I can tell you. But I made up my mind that I wouldn't let those Muddy Creek High kids think they'd beaten me.

Every kid in that lousy class decided it would be a big joke to tease Weird Gina. One by one, they strolled past my desk and made some nasty comment. Or they just sniggered in the mean kind of way that makes you feel like a bit of mouldy old banana that someone has chucked in the gutter.

I could hear those popular kids – Rhonda's new friends – laughing and joking up the back. I just wanted to curl up and die right there in Classroom 1A of Muddy Creek High School. I felt so miserable, I had to fight incredibly hard not to burst into tears. I dug my fingernails into the desk until the fingertips were white. I wouldn't give those kids the satisfaction of seeing me cry.

In case you're wondering, I stuck to my vow, and didn't speak one word to my ex-best friend, Rhonda Goldwyn.

From the back of the classroom, I caught her staring at me with big, sad, puppy-dog eyes. Humph. I didn't care one tiny bit how lousy she was feeling. *She* was the one who'd acted like a rat – not me.

And in the corridor on my way out of that lousy school, Rhonda *tried* to talk to me. She yelled out 'Hi, Gina!' across the hall. I walked straight past as if I couldn't see her and couldn't hear her. Rhonda didn't try to follow me. She knew how stubborn I could be – especially when I'd made a vow. There's no point making vows if you're not going to stick to them.

I could feel Rhonda's puppy-dog eyes boring into my back as I walked away. And I could hear the sound of Kayleen's giggles echoing up and down the corridor.

CHAPTER 8

RUNNING home from the bus-stop, I was crying so much that I could hardly see where I was going. The street and the houses were swimming around in a little sea of tears.

Above my head, dark grey clouds were piling up in the sky, blocking out the sun. All over town, there was that weird, heavy kind of darkness you always get before a big storm. It was as if the sky felt as grim and miserable as I did.

I bawled and blubbered like a little kid all the way home. Rhonda had been my first friend. My only friend. I'd always thought we were the best best friends that had ever been. And now she'd dumped me for those lousy Muddy Creek High kids. It was too terrible to think about. So I stopped thinking about it and just cried instead.

All I could think about was getting home and telling Dad about what had happened. He'd understand. Dad would stick by me. Dad and me had always stuck together (not like that rat, Rhonda Goldwyn).

'I don't need that traitor as a friend, anyway,'

I thought to myself. 'It'll just be Barry and me – like the old days.'

You see, in the old days, when Dad and me were travelling round Australia in The Baked Bean, we did everything together. Just the two of us.

We were on the road then, free and easy, doing whatever we felt like doing. Each night, we'd park the Bean and set up camp somewhere. While we ate our sausages and mash at the little caravan table, we used to talk about what had happened that day and what we wanted to do the next. I used to help Barry out with his inventions and he used to help me to survive school. We had our own special jokes, our own special games and our own special stuff that only we understood.

Some nights we'd go on working in The Baked Bean until really late (way, way after midnight). We'd get so carried away about the invention we were working on that we'd forget how late it was. While we worked, we used to tell each other jokes and laugh and giggle. One of the terrific things about my dad was that he liked being silly almost as much as kids do. He knew how to fool around and have fun without saying 'Don't be silly' like most adults would say. In the old days, we didn't need friends, because we were best mates.

Well, now that I didn't have a best friend any more, it would be back to the old days of Barry and me on our own. I'd race home from school every day to help Dad out in the Invention Workshop. We'd be flat out working on plans and diagrams and marketing strategies. And I *preferred* it that way. I figured we didn't need other people (especially rats like Rhonda Goldwyn). Other people just got in the way. Other people just let you down. I knew that Dad would never let me down.

As I came round the side of our crumbly old house, I saw smoke coming out of the Invention Workshop and the sounds of clattering and hammering inside. Barry must be working on his Musical Bicycle, the G'Day Friendly Alarm Clock, the Auto-Sparkle Shoe Polisher or one of his other new ideas.

I was just busting to blurt out the whole ghastly story about Rhonda. I knew Dad would understand.

I pushed open the door of the Invention Workshop. The first thing I saw was Constable Brenda Snape. The first thing I heard was the sound of Dad and the policewoman laughing. Dad was telling her one of our special jokes and she was helping him work on an invention in the same way I used to do.

Dad looked round with a grin on his face. He could see that my face was all red and blotchy from crying.

'What's up, mate?' he said.

'You don't care! You don't care about me any more either!' I blurted out.

Before Dad could say another word, I ran into the house. I threw myself flat out on my bed like a dead fish and bawled and blubbered even harder than before.

Dad ran inside after me and tried to get me to talk.

'What's the problem, Gina? What's happened to get you into a tizz like this?' he said, doing his Worried Father look.

I wouldn't even look at him. I kept my face buried in my pillow. 'Leave me alone,' I mumbled.

Just at that moment, there was a special kind of rat-a-tat knock on our front door.

'That's Rhonda's knock!' said Dad, grinning like a puppy. 'Rhonda will cheer you up.' And he bounced off to the door. He had no idea how wrong he was.

I could hear Rhonda's voice from the verandah and a minute later, Dad was back.

'Rhonda wants to apologise to you about something, Gina. She said to tell you she's very sorry. The sorriest she's ever been about anything in her whole life.'

'Don't mention that person's name to me,' I snorted, sounding incredibly tough. 'Tell her to rack off.'

'Eh?' gasped Barry, flabbergasted. He didn't have a clue what was going on.

'Just tell Rhonda I hate her guts.'

'But Rhonda's your best friend.'

'Not any more,' I snapped.

'I don't know what's happened between you two, but Rhonda's sorry now. Why don't you just talk to her?' Dad pleaded.

'I made a vow,' I said. 'I swore I wouldn't speak to Rhonda Goldwyn for a million years. If she wants to wait that long, that's her business.'

'Gina, if you could see how sorry Rhonda is, I bet you'd –' he began.

'I made a vow not to speak to her and I'm sticking to it.'

'Look, mate, Rhonda realises she made a mistake,' said Barry, making excuses for that traitor who used to be my best friend. 'Don't hold it against her.'

'I *do* hold it against her and I'll *never* forgive her.' (I can be stubborn when I want to be.)

'Come on, Gina,' Barry persevered, 'best friends like you and Rhonda shouldn't be fighting –'

'Yeah? Well, you tell Rhonda Goldwyn that!' I said. 'She's the one who broke our Loyalty Oath. She's the one who acted like a ratfink!'

'Well, Gina, everyone makes mistakes, y'know. If you ask me –' Dad began.

'I'm not asking you! What do you care anyway? Why don't you just go out there and smooch up with that stupid policewoman! Why doesn't everyone just leave me alone!'

And I threw myself out the back door and belted away down the backyard before Dad could stop me.

CHAPTER 9

I HAD never felt so alone in my whole life. I had never felt so crummy and miserable in my whole life either.

I ran away from our house as fast and as far as I could. I never even thought about where I was going. I just wanted to get away from everyone else in the world and be on my own.

A flash of lightning lit up the road like fireworks and a second later there was such a gigantic growl of thunder that it made me jump. The sky was so dark with soggy, black clouds that it was almost like night-time.

I felt a huge plop of rain on my hand. Then a plop on my nose. Another lightning flash seemed to crack open the black clouds and the rain came gushing out. The heaviest rain I'd ever seen. Giant sheets of rain, as if someone was tipping out huge buckets of water from the sky.

In two seconds flat, I was soaked right through to my underwear. There was so much rain in my eyelashes, I could hardly see where I was going.

It was like running through curtains of water hanging in front of me.

For some reason – and I can't really explain why – I ended up running all the way up to the sportsground on the hill outside town. This was one of the special places where Rhonda and me used to hang around together. This was where our Loyalty Oath was buried. We used to sit up on the edge of the oval, with our backs against this huge old ghost-gum and talk until it got dark. It felt incredibly sad to be in our special place and think about all the good times with Rhonda. The good times were over for ever now.

Drenched with rain, the oval was now like a huge lake. I sloshed my way across the squelchy oval and dug the Oath up out of the mud. The rain pelted onto the parchment Rhonda and me had made for the Oath and the ink began to run. All the words of our Oath dissolved and trickled off into the soggy grass. It was the saddest moment of my life.

By the time I got home it was tea-time. I still hadn't figured out what to do. The lights were on in the kitchen – a warm yellow square of light in the middle of the darkness. It looked so cosy and nice, it was enough to make you cry. I stood in the backyard with the rain running down my eyelashes and dripping off my clothes.

Inside, I could see Dad and Brenda Snape cooking sausages and mash for tea. Sausages and mash was always Favourite Tea for me and Dad. We always used to cook it together. I didn't want to go inside. Watching Dad and Constable Snape being all lovey-dovey together made me want to throw up.

I heard a rustle on the grass and then I realised that Constable Snape's horse Zorro was tied up on the back lawn. His glossy black coat glistened with raindrops and I could hear the soft snuffling noise of him breathing.

I pressed myself right up close to Zorro's warm body and stroked his nose. I told him how I felt. I didn't have anyone else I could talk to. At least Zorro listened to me. He nuzzled up against my jumper, making it smell all lovely and horsey.

Then I heard the sound of Dad and Brenda Snape clattering in the kitchen, joking and laughing the way Barry and I used to do. I started to blubber again and let the tears trickle down Zorro's muzzle.

I didn't belong anywhere any more. Rhonda had all her new friends at school and Dad had Constable Snape. No one wanted me around and there was nowhere for me to go.

I realised what I had to do. I had to run away.

It only took me two minutes to come up with my Plan for Running Away. There was no way I could get inside the house to get clothes and stuff without Dad and Brenda Snape hearing me. But I figured it was better to travel light anyway.

The first thing to do was to make sure I had time to make the getaway. I didn't want Dad following me before I had a chance to get far away.

'Dear Dad,' I wrote on a scrap of paper, 'I've decided to forgive Rhonda and be friends with her again. So I'm staying the night at Rhonda's place. Mrs Goldwyn says it's okay. Love, Gina.'

I know this was an enormous lie. I know lying is a terrible thing to do. But, sometimes, when you have to do something important like run away, there's no way of avoiding a few lies.

I slipped the note under the back door, where Barry would be sure to find it. I used to stay the night at Rhonda's heaps of times, so I knew Dad would believe the note and not worry about me.

As quietly as I could, I rolled the Comfee-Cruiser motorised armchair out of the Invention Workshop. I used a piece of strong chain to tie the ComfeeCruiser to the tow-bar of The Baked Bean. Our old caravan had been sitting on the back lawn for so long, I wasn't sure if I could shift it. But I had to try.

I jumped into the ComfeeCruiser and started up the motor. When the motor was revving nicely, I threw it into first gear. The ComfeeCruiser lurched forward. There was a terrible grinding noise as the motor strained to pull the weight of The Baked Bean. It didn't budge one centimetre. The wheels of the caravan had been sitting in the one spot for so long that they'd sunk down into the dirt. Now the rain had turned the ground into a big mud pile and the caravan wheels were bogged.

'Come on, come on,' I whispered to the ComfeeCruiser. 'Give it one more try.'

I gritted my teeth and slammed down the accelerator for one last desperate try. The ComfeeCruiser wheezed and coughed, pulling the chain tight. I felt The Baked Bean rock a bit. It would only take one good shove to get it going, but the ComfeeCruiser motor was going full pelt. It just wasn't going to work.

Then I heard footsteps on the grass. Something bumped against the back of the caravan.

'Uh-oh,' I thought. 'Dad must have heard me. I'm gonna get caught.'

Nervously, I peered through the pelting rain and round the back of the van. It was Zorro. He had his shoulder up against the back end of The Baked Bean, trying to nudge it forward. He wanted to help!

'Thanks, Zorro,' I whispered and leaped back into the soggy motorised armchair. With the ComfeeCruiser motor going flat out and Zorro pushing from behind, we got the caravan inching forward. (I couldn't say for certain that it was Zorro's help that made the difference, but I'd like to *think* it was.)

Slowly, slowly, the armchair dragged the van out of the bog and squelched across our backyard. I turned to wave thanks and goodbye to Zorro as

I steered the ComfeeCruiser and van out on to the dirt road.

We were only going about five centimetres an hour, but I figured once we got level with Mrs Neugebauer's letterbox it was a downhill slope.

I was planning to turn around and have one last look at my house – to say goodbye sort of – but I never got a chance. As soon as the Comfee-Cruiser reached the top of the gentle slope, it started to slide downhill.

I was sopping wet, sitting in a pool of water in the armchair, spattered with mud which sprayed up from the road as we slid down. 'Just as well,' I thought to myself, 'the rain will wash away the tyre marks.' I didn't want anybody following the tracks to find me.

The slope became a little bit steeper and I could feel the weight of the Bean pushing at the back of the ComfeeCruiser. As the van picked up speed downhill, it shoved the armchair forward. We skidded sideways on the slippery mud and wedged against a tree.

At the bottom of the hill was a pretty gully full of ferns where Rhonda and me used to hang out. The ComfeeCruiser and The Baked Bean were now bogged in the middle of the gully. I'd have to stay there until the ground dried out.

Inside the van there was a thick musty smell of a place that's been shut up for ages. It was pitch black inside the van, but I knew my way around so well, it didn't matter. I felt around in the dark to find the old gas lamp and lit it. Everything was dusty and grubby and I thought I saw a spider. But at least there was a bed in there. I was so exhausted, I just wanted to crash out.

I peeled off my wet clothes and wrung them out in the sink. Then I curled up tight on the bed and pulled a dusty old quilt up over me.

I thought back over everything that had happened that day. It just shows you that you can never tell what's going to happen. I mean, one minute I had a best friend and a great father. And the next minute I had no one. Rhonda dumped me for those creeps at school and Barry dumped me for that stupid policewoman.

I know you're not meant to feel sorry for yourself, but I couldn't help it. I'd been crying and blubbering so much, I didn't have any tears left. I just lay there watching the orange gas light flickering against the peeling paint on the ceiling and listening to the rain belting down on the roof of the van.

I hadn't really figured out what to do now that I'd actually run away. But I was too tired to do any serious planning. In the morning, I would decide what to do. All I wanted to do now was go to sleep and forget about everyone and everything.

For a moment, I couldn't stop myself from wondering if anyone would miss me. I figured they wouldn't, since no one cared about me anyway. I was on my own now.

I turned off the gas lamp. In the dark, with the rain drumming on the roof of The Baked Bean, I felt very very very alone. I turned the gas lamp back on and left it burning until the last of the gas had run out.

CHAPTER 10

IT just kept on raining. It rained and rained as if it would never stop. Boy oh boy, was I glad to be safe and dry inside The Baked Bean.

Once, in the middle of the night, I half woke up and heard the giant sheets of rain sploshing against the windows of the caravan. I had this weird feeling that the van was moving. Kind of rocking from side to side gently. I figured I must be dreaming. I snuggled up under the quilt and dozed off again.

Apparently, it wasn't until the morning, when the rain had stopped, that Dad looked out the window and realised The Baked Bean was missing. That's when he got suspicious that maybe I *hadn't* really gone to Rhonda's place. He phoned Rhonda up straight away.

'It sounds to me like Gina's run away, Mr Terrific,' said Rhonda in a Voice of Doom, when Dad told her that the Bean, the ComfeeCruiser and me were all missing.

That's when Dad went into a panic. (He always panics in a crisis. That's why I used to handle things whenever there was a crisis.) He started running around like a headless chook. Constable Brenda Snape said that he should report me as a 'missing person', so he scurried off to the police station.

While Barry was busy panicking and filling out heaps of forms at the police station, Rhonda was busy thinking. She was worried about me too, but no matter how worried Rhonda gets, her brain keeps ticking over.

Rhonda thought about all the places I might have gone. And then she thought about how heavy the caravan was and how you couldn't drag it very far with a motorised armchair. Rhonda put two and two together.

'Downhill!' thought Rhonda, with one of her brainwaves. 'She must have gone to the gully, downhill from the house.'

Rhonda sloshed and tramped her way through the mud down to the pretty gully full of ferns behind our house. The only trouble was, there weren't any ferns in the gully any more. There was no sign of The Baked Bean in the gully. There was a river.

The night before, buckets of rain whooshed down all the hills around Borrington. All the little gullies became little streams. And all the little streams poured down into the big gully behind our house. So now it was a river. The geography teacher at Muddy Creek High reckoned it was a 'flash flood'.

Rhonda didn't have to know anything about flash floods to work out what had happened. She saw the muddy tyre tracks on the banks of the new river and she realised that The Baked Bean must be somewhere downstream.

Of course, when I got up that morning, I didn't know anything about Rhonda looking for me or Dad filling out Missing Person forms. I didn't think they cared about me at all.

A flash of bright sunlight through a gap in the caravan curtains woke me up. The sky was as brilliantly blue as the sky in cartoons. It was hard to believe it had rained so much during the night. It took me a minute to remember I was in The Baked Bean and another minute to remember that I'd run away. I tied the quilt around myself and pulled back the curtains to look out the van window.

The gully looked different. For a start, the gum trees seemed to be moving. The Baked Bean bumped up against something and rocked sideways.

Then I realised: it wasn't the trees that were moving. The Baked Bean was moving. Floating.

I tried to open the caravan door but it was jammed tight. A trickle of water oozed in from the edge of the door. The door was half under water.

Instead, I climbed up on the sink and opened the roof hatch. Hoisting myself through the hatch, I had a good view all around The Baked Bean.

The mighty Bean was scudding along a small creek. The banks of this creek had trees growing right up out of the water, where the rain had swamped paddocks the night before. The water wasn't very deep but it was fast, swirling past rocks and broken tree branches. As well as the caravan, lots of other junk was scooting along for the ride – bits of trees, old planks, car tyres, plastic ice-cream containers – all kinds of stuff.

I guess it's pretty hard to believe that a caravan could float down a river like that, without tipping over or sinking. Well, there's a perfectly logical reason.

You see, a couple of years ago, when Barry and me were still travelling around Australia, Dad had one of his Brilliant Ideas. He thought it would be a good idea to invent an amphibious caravan – that is, a caravan that could go on dry land *and* on water. He figured a holiday would be more fun if you could unhook your caravan from a car, hook it up to a boat and cruise off somewhere. He called it the Terrific Caraboat.

Anyway, Barry experimented with The Baked Bean for a while. He constructed a new waterproof hull for the van's underbelly, added stabilisers (like they have in houseboats), and tinkered with a steering mechanism. Then he got excited about some other invention and forgot all about the Caraboat idea. (That's typical of my dad. He's always rushing off in three directions at once.)

Well, now the Bean was an amphibious vessel whether I liked it or not, and I was certainly glad that I wasn't about to sink.

A piece of flowery material that looked familiar floated past. It was part of the upholstery on the ComfeeCruiser. There was no sign of the motorised armchair in front of the caravan, so I figured it had come loose during the night. The poor old ComfeeCruiser must be smashed up on the rocks somewhere upstream.

Up ahead, the water seemed to widen out all of a sudden. I was craning my neck to see round a clump of trees in front, when I felt the van lurch sideways. I lost my balance and fell into the sink. I scrambled back through the hatch just in time to see The Baked Bean (with me on board of course) being sucked out of the little creek and into a big proper river.

This river, swollen with the water from all the flooded creeks, had swallowed up the land on both banks, including whole forests of trees. The water was flowing so fast that it made a dull roaring sound and, through the floor of the van, I could feel the power of the river dragging me along. I crossed my fingers that the waterproof hull Barry invented would hold up.

Just then I saw someone on the left bank of the river. It was a kid, about eight years old, fishing. With his fishing rod, he was trying to hook some of the junk that scooted past.

As you can imagine, when he saw a caravan on the river, with a person sticking out through the roof, he looked pretty surprised.

'Are you okay?' he bellowed across the water.

'I think so!' I yelled back.

'Need a hand?'

'No thanks!' I shook my head. 'Can you tell me where I am?'

'In a caravan!' yelled the kid. Boy, do I hate smartarses.

'What river is this?' I persisted.

'The Widgee Widgee River. Coupla kilometres south of Oodnaroonga.'

'Where's that?' I asked, but The Baked Bean was sailing along so quickly, I was too far past the kid. He couldn't hear me.

I plonked myself back down through the hatch into the van to consider the situation.

On one hand, I had a lot to be terrified about. I was alone in a runaway caravan on a flooded river with no idea where I was. At the moment, I didn't have any way to steer or stop the floating Bean. On the other hand, the van seemed to be waterproof and was sailing along pretty well so far.

Yes! I decided that this was in fact a monster stroke of luck. The flood had made the decision for me! (That is, the decision about what to do now that I'd run away.)

I would sail The Baked Bean as far as it would take me. Far away from Borrington and ratfink ex-best friends and fathers who fell in love with policewomen. Maybe if I kept following rivers, I'd end up coming out into the sea. Then I could travel by boat or train or camel or whatever I could find, all over the world.

I would wander the world having adventures, but always on my own. No one would ever know the full story about why I was wandering the world and I would never say too much about myself. I would be tough and cool and aloof – never making friends or letting anyone get close to me. A loner. A lone eagle.

People would see me in Bagdad or Rio de Janeiro or in the middle of Siberia and say 'Who is that mysterious girl wandering the world on her own?' And other people would say 'We don't know who she is. But she looks so sad. Obviously something tragic happened to her in the past and now she travels around all alone.'

That was it! For the rest of my life, I would be a Tragic Girl of Mystery wandering the world!

CHAPTER 11

THE trouble was, a Tragic Girl of Mystery wasn't going to get far in some muddy clothes with no food. I decided to make an inventory of the supplies I had and a list of the supplies I needed to get. Luckily, there was a scribble pad and some pens in one of the drawers.

SUPPLIES NEEDED
1) Maps – Widgee Widgee River
   New South Wales rivers
   The World
2) Clothes
3) Food
4) Gas (for the gas lamp and the stove)
5) Fresh water

I had a good hunt around the van, poking in all the cupboards and drawers and gadgets Barry had built years ago. Most stuff had been cleared out and a lot of what was left I had to chuck out because it was mouldy.

SUPPLIES AVAILABLE
1) 1 scribble pad and 3 pens
2) 2 small tins of baked beans
3) 1 packet instant custard powder
4) various tools and gadgets
5) 1 school uniform and underwear, muddy
6) 1 pair of school shoes, wet
7) $\frac{1}{2}$ a muesli bar, soggy (This had been in the pocket of my school uniform, left over from lunch the day before.)
8) 2 candles
9) $ 2.42

Hmm...I certainly needed a lot of supplies. Obviously $2.42 wouldn't go very far. Eventually, I'd have to find a way to earn some money. But in the meantime, what could I do for food and stuff? There was no way I could avoid it – I'd have to *steal* some food.

I felt pretty crummy about the idea of stealing. I'd never stolen anything in my whole life. But this was an emergency. I decided that I would make a list of all the stuff I stole and then post the money back to the people I'd stolen from later on. I felt much better once I'd worked out that plan.

I pulled on my school uniform ready to face the world. The uniform was all stiff and crumbly with the dried-on mud but it was the best I could do.

The school shoes were too soggy and heavy to bother with.

All of a sudden an enormous thump rocked The Baked Bean, sending me flying across and smack-bang into the wardrobe. It felt like we'd stopped.

From the roof hatch, I looked out to see that the van was jammed in a bend in the river. An old mattress and some other junk was tangled up around the trunk of a huge tree that had fallen into the river. The Bean had collided with the pile of junk and was wedged there. Another stroke of luck! This was my chance to anchor the van to the bank.

It's amazing the things a person will do when they *have* to. I mean, there are moments when a person is concentrating so hard on getting a thing done, that they forget to be scared. Well, that's exactly what happened to me.

On my tummy, I slid down the round front end of the Bean. I managed to land with my feet on the tow-bar. I wobbled and swayed like crazy and, with the river swirling around my feet, I was sure I'd fall in. I had to cling tightly on to the tow-bar with my toes like a monkey.

The length of chain I'd used to tow the van the night before was still attached to the tow-bar. I scooped it up out of the water and jumped into the river. It came up to my waist and I could feel the strong current tugging at me. Panting with the effort, I managed to wade across to the bank and tie the end of the chain to the sturdiest looking tree.

Phew...I'd done it: anchored the Bean safely. I collapsed onto the grassy bank, dripping wet and out of breath.

Obviously, I was going to have to find easier ways to steer and stop the Bean. As I lay there in a soggy heap, I could see a metal thing sticking out of the water at the back end of the van. Then I remembered! Dad had tinkered with a rudder for the Terrific Caraboat! He never got round to finishing it, but part of the mechanism was still there.

I clambered back onto the pile of junk and fished around. I thought an old metal garden spade and a hunk of wire might do the trick. Using the wire, I tied the spade onto the metal stump that Barry had left sticking out the back end of the van.

Inside the van, I found where the other end of the metal stump came out: behind the mattress on the bed there was a lever that Dad had left half-finished. By turning the lever, I could manoeuvre the spade in the water, like a rudder. It wasn't perfect, but it would have to do as a way to steer the Bean.

I needed an anchor too. That was easier. On the bank, a little way downstream, an old petrol gerry can had been washed up. I filled it full of river stones and tied it onto the chain on the van tow-bar. The petrol can made a perfect anchor.

This inventing brainwork took some time and my stomach told me it was getting close to lunchtime. I needed to go ashore and find food.

There was not a house in sight for kilometres in any direction. A rough dirt road ran alongside the river, but it didn't seem to lead anywhere. I'd practically given up when I saw a ramshackle petrol station in the middle of nowhere with a house a bit further away surrounded by hedges.

When I say 'petrol station', I really mean one rusty, ancient petrol pump and a corrugated iron shed. Through the smear of dirty grease on the window, I could just make out a man inside.

'G'day,' I said, trying to look relaxed.

'G'day,' said the bloke, wiping his black greasy hands on a greasy rag.

'Mind if I fill up these water bottles?' I asked, holding up two big plastic containers.

'Help yourself, love,' he said.

While I held the bottles under the tap, I could feel the petrol bloke watching me carefully, taking a good look at my muddy uniform and bare feet. I tried hard not to look suspicious.

'Camping out, are ya?' he asked, looking me up and down with his squinty eyes.

'Umm, yeah – me and my dad pitched our tent back there a bit,' I lied.

'Aww yeah?' he said, sounding very suspicious. 'What brings you round this way in the middle of a flood?'

'Umm…' I had to think quickly, 'we're look-ing for my uncle. He lives somewhere around here. Is that your house?' I asked, pointing to the house hidden behind its hedges, about two hundred metres away. (It was the only house within cooee and my only chance of getting supplies, I figured.)

'Nah, love.'

'Maybe that's my uncle's place,' I said, looking for an excuse to go over there.

'Boris Crump?' said the petrol bloke, screwing up his face in a weird sort of way.

'Yeah, that's him – Uncle Boris,' I lied some more.

'Does he know you're coming?'

'Umm, no – it's a surprise,' I fibbed.

'Ooh, *you* might be the one who's in for a surprise, love,' he said, sucking the air through his teeth. 'That Boris Crump's a bit of a solitary bugger. He doesn't like visitors. Doesn't like them at all. Keeps out of everybody's way. I haven't even laid eyes on him for the last fifteen years I've been working here. Hey – where exact-ly are you and your dad camped?'

This petrol pump bloke was starting to ask too many questions for my liking. I told him a few more lies and pretended I was in a hurry. Inside the tin shed, the only maps he had for sale were pretty grubby, with smears of car grease all over them. But I didn't have much choice. I bought a map of New South Wales and two boxes of

77

matches for $2.05. (That left me with 37c.)

Leaning up against his rusty, greasy petrol pump, the bloke watched me walk over to the house where my 'Uncle Boris' lived. There were high, thick hedges all around the house which, luckily, meant that the nosy petrol bloke couldn't see me any more.

This Boris Crump certainly didn't seem enthusiastic about visitors. Inside the hedge, there was a brick fence with bits of broken bottles cemented along the top edge. The jagged points of glass glinted in the sunlight like vicious teeth. Inside the brick fence was a lower barbed wire fence, with extra barbed wire looped round and round it – like you see in war movies.

All around the front gate were signs saying stuff like KEEP OUT and PRIVATE. The biggest sign had red letters about two feet high:

DO NOT ENTER. SHOUT FROM GATE IF
NECESSARY. LEAVE DELIVERIES OUT-
SIDE FENCE.
B. CRUMP.

I was feeling pretty curious about this Mr Crump. Maybe he was a Tragic Man of Mystery. I mean, maybe some terrible thing happened to him (for example, his best friend doing the dirty on him). And that was why he wanted to be on his own (like me).

Anyway, I couldn't let the fences or the signs

78

put me off. I needed supplies urgently and I figured that, no matter how weird or unsociable he was, Boris Crump would have some clothes and food somewhere.

Round the side, I found a loop of barbed wire that I could fit through. I left the water containers outside and picked my way through the fence slowly and carefully. There didn't seem to be any sign of Mr Crump as I crept into the backyard.

I was heading towards the back of the house when I felt my foot trip over a wire. Next thing I knew, an alarm went off, shrieking loud enough to burst a person's eardrums. I froze like a wallaby caught in the beam from car headlights. The shrill 'wahoo-wahoo' of the alarm shot through my head as I looked for somewhere to hide.

Suddenly there was silence. Someone had switched off the alarm. Through the screen door mesh, I saw Boris Crump peering out into the backyard. The silence was broken by the thwack of the screen door being snapped open.

'Get out of it!' he snarled. But not at me. With my back flat against the wall of the house, I was safely hidden.

Boris Crump was wearing army combat clothes – the kind of blotchy jungle camouflage gear that people buy in disposal stores. I was surprised to see that Mr Crump wasn't a really old crochety man like I'd imagined. He was about the same age as my dad (old but not really old). I wondered what had happened in his life to make him want to be a cranky hermit.

'I know you're out there, ya bloody mongrels!' he growled. (Maybe at dogs – I couldn't tell.) He turned the hose on full blast and ran off down the yard with it, spraying it like a machine gun at whatever 'mongrels' he might find.

This was my chance to duck inside and grab some food quick smart. While Mr Crump was patrolling with the hose at the other end of his yard, I dashed into the house. I knew it was risky, but I was desperate for something to eat by now.

Everything in the kitchen was squeaky, shiny clean, and completely bare, as if no one lived there. All the cupboards seemed to be empty. I yanked open the door of the freezer and saw it was chockablock with frozen dinners. Stacked right to the top with packets of 'Solo Dinner For One' and 'Just-For-One Instant Dinner'.

It seemed kind of sad to think of Mr Crump defrosting the frozen dinners to eat all on his own.

I stuffed one packet into the pocket of my school uniform and piled up another half a dozen packets in my arms. It was better than nothing. Then I looked around for paper to write an I.O.U. note. For a moment, I thought I heard the squeak of the screen door hinge, but I figured it was my imagination.

CHAPTER 12

'DROP those frozen dinners – *now*!' boomed a voice right behind me.

I dropped the stack of frozen dinners onto the floor with a loud thud, then slowly turned around.

Boris Crump had the hose aimed at me like a gun. So I put my hands up in the air like people do in the movies.

'I'm sorry...it's just that I'm very hungry and I –' I started to explain.

'Can you read, kid?' snarled Mr Crump.

I nodded nervously.

'Well, didn't you see the signs out the front to keep out?'

'I saw them,' I murmured.

'I just want to be left alone! Is that too much to ask? Do I come around to your house and bother you?' yelled Boris Crump.

'No.'

'Well, why don't you just leave me alone! I just want people to *keep away*! Like the signs out the front say! Do you understand, kid?' he raved on, so revved up his face was bright red and blotchy.

'I do understand actually,' I said. 'I mean, I understand about wanting to be on your own and everything. I suppose something terrible happened to you that made you want –'

For some reason, this made Mr Crump even angrier. His red face kind of exploded like an over-ripe tomato and he let out a gigantic roar.

'Get out! Get outta my house, kid!'

So I did. As fast as I could. Running like a scared rabbit. I was too scared to look back as I belted out the back door.

Then I felt something thwack me hard in the back. Boris Crump turned his hose on me. The spray of the water was like a slug in the guts, drenching me and throwing me right off balance.

I could hardly see where I was going in the spray of water, with Mr Crump yelling 'Get out!' behind me. I scrambled over the barbed wire fence and then the broken glass fence, battered by the blast from the hose. The barbed wire grazed right along my arm and then I heard the rip of my uniform on a piece of broken glass. I tripped over the water containers and sprawled face first in the gravel.

Back out on the street, I stopped to put down the heavy water containers and catch my breath. Only then did I realise there was a stinging, burning pain on my right leg. The broken glass had ripped through the bottom edge of my uniform and made a jagged cut, about eight centimetres long, just above my knee.

I'm usually pretty tough about blood and gory

things in general. But I have to admit that when I lifted up the blood-stained skirt and saw the gash on my leg, I felt a bit queasy in the guts. Luckily, Mr Crump's hose had washed the cut fairly clean, but I thought I'd better bandage it up to stop the bleeding.

The skirt of my poor old school uniform was badly ripped anyway, so I tore the bottom edge off completely, to use as a bandage.

'Hey!' someone yelled out.

I looked up to see the petrol station bloke watching me.

'Hey, kid! Where did you say your father was? You sure he knows where you are? I mean, does he know you're hanging around here? Hey, are you –?'

I didn't hang around to hear any more of his questions. I bolted in to the bush and ran and ran and ran. I must have dropped the torn strip of school uniform on the road near the petrol station but there was nothing I could do about that now.

After a couple of kilometres, my legs kind of buckled up underneath me and I dropped the water containers. The muscles in my legs were wobbling and quivering with exhaustion. I let myself flop down on the grass and doze off to sleep.

A shiver of cold went right through my bones and woke me up eventually. The day had turned chilly while I slept, sprawled out.

By the time I found my way back to The Baked

Bean it was starting to get dark. I clambered inside and plonked myself down on the bed.

I had to admit my first day as a Tragic Girl of Mystery hadn't been a huge success. It felt like every part of my body was hurting. The bottoms of my feet were kind of shredded from running on gravel roads and through the bush. My arm was stinging from the barbed wire, my knees and hands were raw and sore from gravel rash and the cut on my leg was throbbing like crazy. I dabbed at it with antiseptic from the van's first-aid box, but the bandaids had all run out.

The hunger pangs clawing at my tummy were even more painful than the cut on my leg. I hadn't eaten anything since lunchtime the day before. I could hear my stomach snarling and rumbling.

After a whole day, I had fresh water, a map, matches, one Solo Dinner For One and 37c. But I had no gas, food supplies or clothes. It was obvious I was going to have to find other methods for getting supplies.

I'd used up the last of the porta-gas the night before, so I couldn't use the gas lamp. With one of the candles lit, I had just enough light to see what I was doing inside the van.

The first item on my agenda was dinner. Without gas, I couldn't heat anything up, so it would have to be a cold dinner. I peeled the top off the Solo Dinner For One. It was not a pretty sight. Each little compartment of the plastic tray had a congealed mess that had once been food. I suppose it was meant to be a roast dinner, but after thawing out and being shaken around in my pocket, it didn't look much like a roast dinner any more.

I had a taste of the meat, covered in gluggy gluey gravy. Hungry as I was, I had to spit out the one mouthful I tried. The cold, soggy vegetables looked even worse. In fact, I decided that the Solo Dinner For One would probably be disgusting and inedible even if you heated it up properly.

I figured I ought to ration the few supplies I had. I would let myself have one of the tins of baked beans and save the other one for an emergency.

Cold baked beans aren't exactly scrumptious but – let me tell you – I got the lid off that tin faster than you would believe. I gulped down huge spoonfuls of baked beans and before I knew it, the tin was empty.

I was still hungry. But I had to be strong about saving the other tin of baked beans. Who knew when I'd get more food? I had to have will-power.

The candlelight was too dim and the map was too smudgy with grease to see it properly. And anyway, I wasn't really in the mood to look at maps and make plans. I was feeling pretty low.

Looking at the gluggy mess of the Solo Dinner For One in the garbage bin, I couldn't help thinking about Boris Crump. Even after what had happened, you couldn't help feeling sorry for a bloke like that. I'd never know what had turned him into a Tragic Man of Mystery, but it must have been something pretty dreadful.

Someone or lots of someones must have hurt Mr Crump's feelings so badly that he just wanted to hide away from the whole world and be on his own. I could understand that. I mean, if you couldn't trust a best friend when you'd signed a Loyalty Oath in blood, then I didn't reckon there was anybody in the world you could trust. It was better not to rely on anyone and get by on your own. A loner. Mr Crump had the right idea.

Then again, it seemed to me that loners didn't *have* to be grouchy old buggers like Boris Crump. I mean, there were two ways a Tragic Person of Mystery could operate: (1) you could turn nasty like Boris Crump (turning hoses on people, putting barbed wire around your house, etc.) or (2) you could be a *polite* Tragic Person of Mystery, wandering around the world keeping to yourself, but trying not to hurt other people's feelings.

I definitely wanted to operate the second way. I never wanted to trust anyone ever again, but that didn't mean I wanted to be grouchy.

All this thinking made me even hungrier. I caved in and ate the other tin of baked beans. As soon as I'd finished it (in about two seconds flat) I felt cranky with myself for not having any will-power.

Maybe it was a combination of hunger, exhaustion and my injuries, or maybe it was because of the flickering light from the one candle in the dark caravan. But, whatever the reason, I started to have weird thoughts – kind of hallucinations. I started to remember stuff so clearly that it was like I really saw them in the caravan. Stuff from the old days when Dad and me lived in The Baked Bean travelling around together. For example, I remembered the day Dad first showed me the bed he'd invented for me – a special bed which unwound from the ceiling of the van with a little ladder for me to climb in. (It was all rusted up now.) I remembered all the nights we cooked sausages and mash on the little gas stove, singing silly songs and telling each other jokes. The memory was so strong, I could just about hear the sausages sizzling and smell them too.

The imaginary smell of sausages brought on another pang of hunger. The memories vanished and I reminded myself that I was alone, hungry, wounded, with no friends any more. My dad was in love with that stupid policewoman and didn't care about me anyway. So there was no point remembering that stuff and being sooky about it.

In fact, one of the most important things a Tragic Girl of Mystery has to do is learn not to be sooky about anyone or anything. No matter how miserable it felt to be lonely, I had to get used to it. That was all part of being a Tragic Girl of Mystery.

CHAPTER 13

WEIRD rumbling noises woke me up early the next morning. It took me a few minutes to work out that it was my own stomach making those growling noises. I was so hungry I could have eaten half a dozen soggy defrosted Solo Dinners For One.

But hunger wasn't my only problem. As I swung out of bed, I felt my bare feet hit something wet and cold on the floor. Trickles of water ran across the floor and formed a puddle near the gas stove. Leaks were starting to spring up around the floor of The Baked Bean in the spots where rocks had gouged at the sides of the van.

I had to admit that I'd neglected the Bean up till then. I'd taken for granted Barry's improvements that kept the van afloat. But bits were starting to crack or fall apart. If I didn't do some urgent maintenance straight away, there was a risk my floating caravan might sink.

I added 'Tools and materials to repair Bean' to my list of Supplies Needed. According to my map, the next town along the Widgee Widgee River was Possum Hill. I figured Possum Hill would be the place for me to 'borrow' some food and other supplies.

Once I saw the rooftops of the town up ahead, I looked for a spot to anchor The Baked Bean. There was a little bend with willow trees over-hanging the water and, with my new spade-rudder, I steered the van towards it. Once the Bean was anchored in the bend and tied to a tree trunk, the willow branches draped over it right down to the water. You would hardly know there was a caravan there.

Picking my way through the bush and into town, I was a bit worried that my torn, muddy school uniform, bare feet and gashed leg might make me look a bit conspicuous. But Possum Hill turned out to be a tiny, sleepy town with no one around. It only had one pub, a sub-post office and a couple of shops. Luckily for me, one of those shops was Brian and Val's Hardware and Building Supplies.

As I went inside the store, my heart was thump-ing very hard and my cheeks were burning bright red. I looked incredibly guilty before I'd even done anything wrong. You see, apart from Mr Crump's frozen dinner, I had never stolen any-thing in my whole life. Some kids at Muddy Creek High thought that shoplifting was cool. They used to try and impress each other by nick-ing stuff from the local shops. Rhonda always used to say that shoplifting was just a very dumb way for childish kids to show off. I agreed with her and I still do. But let's face it, I was desperate (that is, nearly fainting from hunger and with my van about to sink). If I took just what I really needed and paid the shop back later, that wouldn't be so bad. That's what I told myself anyway.

There didn't seem to be anyone behind the counter. This was almost too good to be true. If I was quick, I'd be able to 'borrow' the things I needed and slip away without anyone even knowing I was there.

The hardware store was chockablock with racks and shelves and plastic bins jumbled up with tools, nuts and bolts, paint, fencing wire and all the little doodads that hardware stores sell. I darted around, taking only the things I really needed, and stuffed them in an old shopping bag.

I was standing in front of the Boat Supplies shelf, looking for some waterproofing stuff, when I heard a shuffle behind me.

I spun around to see who it was.

'Oh, hello,' I said, trying to sound as sweet and innocent as I could.

Behind the counter was a kid about the same age as me, wearing a bright blue wetsuit. He had the kind of dark brown tan and bleached stringy hair that people get when they lie around on a beach all day. There was a smear of Pinke Zinke across his nose and a full-sized surfboard resting inside the crook of his arm. If it weren't for the fact that Possum Hill was 250 kilometres inland, you'd swear he'd just stepped off the beach at Bondi.

The Kid With the Surfboard was staring at me with an incredibly sulky look on his face. 'How long had he been standing there watching me?' I wondered. 'Had he seen me nick the other stuff?'

'D'you wanna buy some boat supplies?' he said at last.

'Oh...umm...I'm not sure what kind I should get,' I muttered, slipping a tube of waterproof sealant into my pocket.

'Have you got a boat?' asked the Kid With the Surfboard.

'A boat? Well, sort of...'

I was busting to ask him why he was carrying a surfboard since we were 250 kilometres from the sea. But I figured that if I didn't ask him too many questions, he wouldn't ask me any. I needed to get out of that hardware store quick smart. I found my last 37c in my pocket.

'I'll just buy these today,' I said, grabbing a handful of screws and plonking them on the counter.

'That'll be 35c,' said the Kid, peering at me through his blond straw fringe.

'Thanks,' I said and ducked out of the shop.

I couldn't believe I'd actually got away with it. But right down in the pit of my stomach, I felt a big lump of guilt eating away at me. On my scribble pad, I wrote out an I.O.U. – a list of all the things I'd taken from the shop – and signed it Tragic Girl of Mystery. I slipped the note through the side door of Brian and Val's Hardware and Building Supplies.

I didn't like the suspicious way that Kid With the Surfboard had looked at me, so the sooner I got back to The Baked Bean the better.

The Bean was safely tucked away in its willow tree hiding place. I dropped my bag of loot from the hardware store into the van and was about to climb out again to go in search of food.

'That's not a boat!' someone yelled out from the bank.

Uh-oh. I stuck my head out the window to see the Kid from the hardware store standing beside the willow tree, holding his surfboard and a small backpack. He'd changed out of the wetsuit into fluorescent green board shorts and a tropical shirt.

'You followed me!' I said indignantly.

'Only because you said you had a boat,' he said. 'That's not a boat. That's just a crummy old caravan. That's crummy.'

'Well, I didn't ask you to follow me down here. This just happens to be a fabulous floating caravan, for your information,' I replied, defending the Bean. 'Why don't you just rack off!'

'I saw you steal a bag full of stuff from my mum and dad's hardware store. I could dob you in as easily as that,' he snapped his fingers.

Hmm. I'd better play this cool. The Kid With the Surfboard had me in a tight spot, that was for sure.

'What do you want then?' I asked.

'Does that old rustbucket really float?'

'It's not 'an old rustbucket'. And yes it floats. It's an amphibious vessel,' I said, trying to keep my temper.

'Let me come on board. I'll do you a deal.'

A deal – ha! I'd always thought that Rhonda and I had a deal to be friends for ever and look what happened. I didn't believe in deals any more. But, in this case, I didn't have much choice.

The Kid climbed in through the roof hatch, hauling his surfboard with him.

'Where are you headed for?' he asked.

'That's my business,' I said mysteriously.

'Well, it's my business too now.' He was trying to sound tough. 'Do you reckon this thing could get all the way to the coast?'

'Sure.'

'Well, I want to get to the coast,' said the Kid With the Surfboard. 'If you let me travel with you in this caravan as far as the coast, I promise I won't dob you in for stealing the stuff. That's the deal.'

'That's blackmail,' I pointed out.

'I s'pose it is. But I've gotta get to the coast somehow.'

I certainly didn't want a passenger. Especially some goofy boy with a surfboard. But I was heading for the coast anyway and I couldn't risk getting caught for stealing.

'Okay, it's a deal,' I said reluctantly.

'Beaudie,' he grinned, holding out his hand for me to shake. 'By the way, my name's Waxhead. You haven't told me your name.'

'Well, I don't reckon you need to know my name.'

'I've gotta call you something,' Waxhead insisted.

'Hmm...well, I guess you can call me the Girl of Mystery.'

'Aww, I'm not gonna call you that. I'd feel stupid. That's stupid.'

'Look,' I snapped, 'I reckon there are a few things we need to get straight. I don't want you on my caravan in the first place. Just because we're going to travel together, doesn't mean we have to like each other, okay? The only thing you need to know about me is that I'm a loner – I don't have any friends. I don't trust anyone. So I don't trust you. You don't trust me. Okay?'

'Okay,' Waxhead shrugged. 'All I care about is getting to the coast.'

'That's another thing,' I said, keeping up the tough act. 'If we're going to get this caravan to the coast, there's a lot of maintenance that needs to be done. I expect you to do your share of the work.'

'Sure,' said Waxhead. 'But let's get moving, eh? I wanna get a fair way down the river before anyone realises I'm gone.'

'Before we go anywhere, we have to plan the route,' I said, spreading the map out on the table.

'What a crummy map,' whinged Waxhead.

'Are you going to whinge about everything?' I snapped. It was true that the map was pretty crummy – covered in blobs of grease and black smudges from the filthy petrol station. In a lot of places, you couldn't read what was underneath the smudges. But it was good enough to work out the quickest route from Possum Hill to the coast. If we travelled down the Widgee Widgee River a bit further, then we could branch south into the Bodgee Bodgee River and follow it all the way to the sea.

I took a step back from the map and – thunk! I hit my head on something. I turned around to see Waxhead's dirty great surfboard with its red fin looming over me. He had leaned his board against the van cupboards and it took up most of the spare room inside the little caravan.

'You can't keep this thing inside,' I said, sounding pretty tough.

'Where else is it going to go?' asked Waxhead, stroking his precious surfboard as though it was a puppy or something.

'Outside,' I said. 'We can tie it onto the back of the van.'

'No way!' he shouted. 'My board stays with me!'

'Look,' I snapped. 'You may have hijacked

this floating caravan but I'm still the captain of this vessel. What I say goes.'

Waxhead crinkled up his lips in an annoyed sort of way and glared at me. He made a big deal out of it, as if I was acting in an incredibly nasty way. But actually, I reckon he agreed with me. He could see the surfboard took up too much room inside the Bean. It was only logical to move it outside.

We tied his board onto the back of the van and, once we got moving, it scudded along behind us nicely, like a little dinghy. Waxhead rushed to the back window every five minutes to check it was okay. He couldn't really relax whenever his surfboard was out of his sight.

'C'mon. Let's get this rustbucket moving,' said Waxhead hopping around nervously.

And so we set sail – a kid with a weird name, a surfboard that was taller than he was, and a Tragic Girl of Mystery (me) – heading for the open sea.

CHAPTER 14

'HEY, Girl of Mystery – are you hungry?' asked Waxhead, as he unpacked his haversack.

'Oh – a bit,' I lied, trying not to sound too desperate.

'I just grabbed all this stuff from the pantry before I nicked off,' he explained, laying out two packets of biscuits, a tin of ham, three chocolate bars and a few cartons of yoghurt. 'It's not much, but I can add it to what you've already got, eh?'

'Umm...actually...' I stammered. 'I'm out of food. And gas. And money.'

'Yeah? You're a pretty pathetic Girl of Mystery, aren't ya?' said Waxhead. I was sick of this kid complaining all the time and I was about to do my block when he said 'No worries' and hauled a china money-box in the shape of a surfboard out of his haversack, and rattled it. 'My life savings.'

We emptied out all the coins onto the caravan table and counted, while I chomped on as many biscuits as I could without looking disgusting.

'$26.74,' Waxhead announced triumphantly. 'That'll buy enough food and gas to get us as far as the coast, don't ya reckon?'

'I'll only use this money on the condition that I pay you back my half once I've made my fortune,' I insisted. I didn't want to owe anybody anything.

'Okay,' he shrugged. 'Doesn't bother me either way.'

I felt a *lot* better once I had some food in my tummy and ready to start work on the van. Waxhead and me worked flat out for the rest of that day, to make sure The Baked Bean was shipshape for our long voyage. The first job was to plug any holes in the floor and walls, and to waterproof the leaky bits.

I was determined to keep my mouth shut (to stay mysterious). I didn't want to tell this kid anything about myself. This was pretty hard work for me, because I'm usually such a motor-mouth. But Waxhead was keen to talk so I just listened while he yabbered away about his problems. I didn't mind, because I was dead curious about him. For a start, I was busting to know how he'd ended up with a name like 'Waxhead'.

It turned out that he got nicknamed 'Waxhead' because he was such a surfing freak. (You see, surfers coat their surfboards with wax.) His real name was Brian McKellen Junior, but he said if I ever called him 'Brian' he'd thump me.

Waxhead lived all his life at Crystal Beach and

he'd been a surfing freak ever since he could remember. He got his first surfboard when he was four years old. He used to go surfing before school, after school, every weekend – summer and winter. All his mates were surfers and all he ever thought about was surfing.

Waxhead's troubles had started on the day, three months before, when his parents announced the whole family was moving. Mr and Mrs McKellen decided to leave Crystal Beach and buy the hardware store at Possum Hill. Waxhead would be 250 kilometres from the beach. He'd have to give up surfing and give up all his surfing mates.

'Surfing is my whole life, y'know,' was how Waxhead explained it to me. So when they moved, it was like his whole life was over. Waxhead had tried to explain this to his parents. He'd tried to persuade them to let him stay at the coast, but they didn't listen.

'Ever since I was a little kid, I've wanted to be a champion surfer, y'know,' Waxhead said, and you could tell he really meant it. 'I don't treat surfing like some little kid's game. I take it seriously. I used to practise every day. I was winning all the Junior events in the local surfing competitions. I had my sights set on the nationals and then the international surfing circuit.'

But Waxhead's parents didn't understand that. They were the kind of parents who don't take into account what a kid thinks and what a kid might want to do. Mr and Mrs McKellen thought Waxhead would forget about surfing once they moved to Possum Hill. They thought he'd 'grow out of it'.

'They just don't understand me,' Waxhead sighed.

So, from the day they moved to Possum Hill, Waxhead carried his surfboard with him everywhere. He took it into the classroom with him. He even hauled it into bed with him. It was an Act of Protest.

But Waxhead's surfboard protest, plus all his arguing and lots of heavy-duty sulking, hadn't made any difference. His parents just wouldn't listen. Waxhead got so desperate he decided to run away. So when he saw me looking at the boat supplies that morning, he thought it was his chance. He was determined to get back to the beach, back to his surfing mates, back to the thing he cared about most in the whole world – surfing.

I felt pretty sorry for Waxhead once I heard his story. I could understand why he'd decided to run away. When I heard about parents like Mr and Mrs McKellen, it made me feel lucky that Barry was a really different kind of father. I mean, most parents don't think kids have any rights at all.

'My dad's not like that,' I couldn't help boasting. 'My dad reckons that when a family has to make a decision about something, then the kids should have an equal say.'

'Yeah? You reckon your dad wouldn't make

you move somewhere you didn't want to go?'

'Well...it would depend,' I explained. 'We'd talk about it and make a decision together. Like partners.'

'Yeah?' said Waxhead, obviously impressed. 'I'd love to have parents like that. Dead-set.'

Piles of junk were still floating downriver – stuff that had been damaged and then washed downstream by the floodwaters. Half-sunk boats, tangled heaps of timber and fibro, bits of cars, a sofa, a fridge and several bicycles. Believe it or not, with all the other debris scudding along, The Baked Bean didn't look as conspicuous as you might imagine. No one was too surprised to see an old caravan floating through all the other broken, forgotten things.

Waxhead and I found some useful bits and pieces on one of the floating islands of junk: all kinds of doodads that came in handy for fixing up the van.

We stopped for a lunch break (a yoghurt each and more biscuits) and then we kept on working. There was lots to do. The next job was to over-haul all the gadgets and contraptions inside the Bean and try to get them working again. The Ezy-Stir Automatic Pot Stirrer, the TidyMate Pantry Organiser, the Hide-Away Fold-Up Washing Machine, the MagicScrub Inflatable Bathtub, my special hanging bed and all the other useful gadgets that Dad had installed to make life in the caravan more comfortable.

'Far out!' he gasped. 'Where did you get all this stuff?'

'My dad invented them when we used to live in this caravan all the time. My father's a fabulous inventor.'

With a bit of work and a blob of oil on its hinges, the hanging bed was as good as new. Some of the inventions were so badly rusted up or bashed around that they couldn't be fixed. Some I had to dismantle, find spare parts for, and reassemble. Waxhead didn't seem to know much about mechanical things, so I had to do most of it.

'Hey, where did you learn how to fix things and do all this stuff?' asked Waxhead.

'Dad taught me,' I explained. 'But l can't do half the stuff my dad can do.'

By the time we'd finished, it was nearly midnight. We scoffed the rest of Waxhead's food supply in a midnight feast. I was still trying to keep quiet and not give away any information about myself. I could see Waxhead was dying of curiosity, watching me all the time through his bleached fringe.

'Gee – it's after midnight. My parents never let me stay up this late!' he said.

'My dad used to let me stay up way after midnight if we were working on an invention,' I boasted. And then bit my lip for opening my big mouth too much. Waxhead kept peering at me.

'D'you mind if I ask you a question, Girl of Mystery?'

'Yes, I do. Obviously, I'm a Girl of Mystery. I don't tell anybody anything,' I reminded him.

'You don't have to answer if you don't want to,' Waxhead persisted. 'Is your father dead or something?'

'No,' I said, before I could stop myself.

'Because I was just wondering...if your father is as fantastic as you say, how come you ran away?'

What a stupid question. I clamped my mouth shut and wouldn't answer.

'You have run away, haven't you?'

I didn't want to answer his dumb questions. Especially not about Dad or about why I'd run away.

'I said no questions and I meant it!' I snapped. 'Let's go to sleep. We've got a long way to go tomorrow.'

I climbed into my hanging bed and wound up the ladder. But even after I blew the candles out, Waxhead kept on talking. (What a motor-mouth that kid was – even worse than me.) He raved on and on about his surfing mates – Surfo, Tubehead and Shortie – and about what good friends they all were. He gas-bagged so much about missing his friends, that I just couldn't help thinking about Rhonda.

Rhonda and me had probably been the best

friends that two people could ever be. But everything was ruined now, so there was no point thinking about Rhonda and the good times. I had to shut it out of my brain completely.

'Shut up, will ya! I want to get some sleep, if you don't mind,' I snarled.

'Sorry...just trying to be friendly.'

'Well, *don't*. I told you I don't want to have any friends ever again, and I meant it. *Good night*.'

CHAPTER 15

ONCE we had branched off the Widgee Widgee River and were a few kilometres down the Bodgee Bodgee River, we agreed it was safe enough for us to go ashore for supplies. We were far enough away from Possum Hill that Waxhead wouldn't be recognised.

We anchored the Bean near the next town on our map, a place called Wombat Gully. I was just climbing out of the van when I heard thudding noises behind me. I looked round to see Waxhead hoisting his surfboard ashore.

'You can't bring that with you!' I yelled.

'I take it everywhere,' said Waxhead, popping his head through with the board. 'It's my Act of –'

'Protest. You told me. But you can't bring it now,' I said, amazed that he could be so dopey. 'We are *trying* to be inconspicuous. We are *trying* not to attract attention in this town. What do you reckon people in Wombat Gully are going to think if they see you lugging a surfboard around with you?'

'Oh...I s'pose...' mumbled Waxhead. And, reluctantly, he tied his surfboard back onto the back end of the van. What a dopey guy! I couldn't believe what bad luck I had – here I was stuck travelling with this surfing freak with a water-logged brain.

'Hey, Girl of Mystery,' Waxhead called after me as I hauled the empty gas bottle ashore with me. '*You* look pretty weird, y'know. Dressed like that.'

I looked down at my torn and muddy school uniform. I had to admit he had a point.

Peeking into the backyard of a house on the outskirts of Wombat Gully, I saw what I was looking for. A clothes-line full of clean washing fluttering in the breeze. There didn't seem to be anyone home, so I was able to clamber over the fence and unpeg a turquoise T-shirt and a pair of jeans without anyone seeing. (In my scribble pad, I wrote down the address of the house, so I could post the clothes back when I didn't need them any more.)

I made Waxhead turn his back so I could slip off my tatty old school uniform and pull on the 'borrowed' clothes. The jeans were a bit big, but Waxhead loaned me his belt to keep them up. In a T-shirt, jeans and my school shoes, I looked like any normal kid, and so did Waxhead. No one in Wombat Gully would pay any attention to two normal kids doing a bit of grocery shopping. No one would realise we were desperate fugitives. Or at least, that's what I thought.

We walked up the main street past a few different stores.

'Okay, Waxhead, there's the supermarket over –' I started to say, until I realised Waxhead was hanging around in front of a shop selling TV sets and stereos and stuff.

'Come on!' I growled impatiently. 'We haven't got all day!'

But Waxhead was glued to the TV screens in the shop-window display.

'It's the Hawaii Pro-Classic Surf Comp.!' gasped Waxhead. 'And that's Mitch Maddox! The Greatest Surfer Alive On The Planet!'

I stomped back down the street to where Waxhead stood goggle-eyed at the shop-window full of TV sets.

'Look, bonehead,' I said (and I admit I was very rude), 'I don't think you realise –'

But Waxhead was too revved up to care how nasty I was. 'I'd give anything to be able to surf like that one day! I'm hoping I'll get to meet Mitch Maddox at the Australian Championships next year. Look at that guy handle a wave! Isn't that the most fantastic surfing you've ever laid your eyes on!'

Now, to tell the truth, the surfing was incredibly exciting and more interesting than I thought surfing could be. But there was no way I was going to let that surfing freak know I was interested. Just as I was about to haul him away, the surfing stopped for a commercial break.

'Awww...crummy ads...' mumbled Waxhead.

'Good, let's go,' I snapped, and pointed up the street.

But I couldn't move. Because on five different TV sets lined up in the shop-window was my ex-best friend Rhonda. Eating a Mrs Richard's Country Muffin and pretending to think it was delicious. The local TV station in Wombat Gully was showing the advertisement with Rhonda in it.

I didn't want to watch it. There was no way I wanted to see Rhonda eating that muffin in that stupid commercial. I wanted to run up the street and never see Rhonda's face again. But it felt like my feet were stapled to the footpath. I couldn't *stop* myself watching that TV ad.

And I had to admit that Rhonda was fantastic in it. Her acting was incredibly good and she looked cheeky and funny and nice – like someone you'd love to be friends with.

All the thoughts that I'd been trying not to think came whooshing back into my brain. Thoughts about what good friends Rhonda and me used to be and how everything was wrecked now.

'C'mon, it's just some crummy ad,' whinged Waxhead.

But even when the advertisement was over, I couldn't move. I was frozen to the spot, looking as if I'd seen a poltergeist or something.

108

'Hey, Girl of Mystery – are you okay?' asked Waxhead. 'You look kind of funny. Is something up?'

I wanted to blurt out everything. I wanted to shout out to everyone in the main street of Wombat Gully that that was my ex-best friend on the TV and what a fantastic actress she was. I wanted to blurt out the whole story of how she'd broken our Loyalty Oath and how crummy I felt.

BUT. I was a Tragic Girl of Mystery now. And there was no way Girls of Mystery could confide in anyone. I had to be cool, aloof, mysterious. I could never trust anyone again. This bonehead surfer probably wouldn't understand anyway.

I felt like bursting into tears right there in front of the five TV sets, but I figured Girls of Mystery were too tough to cry. I gritted my teeth together so hard they crunched.

'You get the food supplies and I'll get the porta-gas,' I said. 'Make sure you get everything on this list. Try not to mess it up.' I handed Waxhead the list of groceries we needed, sending him into the little town supermarket. Opposite the supermarket in the main street of Wombat Gully was a service station, and that's where I went to fill up the caravan's portable gas cylinder.

While the service station man was filling up the gas bottle, I hung around the petrol pumps. I was so busy brooding about Rhonda in the TV ad, that at first I didn't notice the lady who kept glaring at me while she waited to get her petrol.

'I'll be with you in a jiffy, Mrs Van der Veen,' said the service station man to the lady waiting beside her car. Mrs Van der Veen wasn't very old, but she seemed so cranky it made her look *older*, if you know what I mean. Her face was tightly crinkled up in a permanent frown. She was particularly cranky about waiting around for her petrol and she hopped from foot to foot impatiently.

'Where did you get that T-shirt?' she said.

'Sorry – are you talking to me?' I asked, as nice as pie.

'I'm not talking to myself, sweetheart,' Mrs Van der Veen said. (Not a very happy person, I thought to myself.) 'I want to know where you got that turquoise T-shirt.'

'My father gave it to me for Christmas,' I lied.

You could tell Mrs Van der Veen wasn't sure whether she should believe me or not. I tried hard not to show how nervous I was and I hoped she couldn't hear my heart thumping. I looked around to see the service station man still filling up the gas – why didn't he hurry? I just wanted to get away from there.

'It looks a lot like a T-shirt of mine.' Cranky Mrs Van der Veen screwed her eyes up suspiciously at me.

'Isn't that a coincidence?' I said, hoping it didn't sound *too* pathetic.

Across the road, I could see Waxhead paying for the groceries at the checkout.

'That'll be $7.50 for the gas, pet,' said the service station man, bringing back the gas bottle.

I was just counting out the money when Mrs Van der Veen suddenly threw the car keys onto the bonnet of her car. 'Hey! They're my jeans and that's definitely my T-shirt!'

She flew across the concrete and grabbed me in a wrestle hold.

'Call the police. These are stolen clothes!' she barked at the service station bloke.

The man looked baffled, as if he wasn't sure what to do. Across the road, Waxhead was watching this little scene. He could tell I was in big trouble.

'I'll phone the police myself,' she said crossly. 'Just keep a hold of her.' She handed her prisoner (me) over to the bewildered service station bloke, marched to the telephone and started dialling.

I wondered what Waxhead was thinking. Maybe he would be pleased if I got caught. Then he could take The Baked Bean and travel to the coast without me hanging around. I'd been pretty mean to him and he didn't owe me anything, that was for sure. I tried to work out the expression on his face but he was too far away.

Suddenly he collapsed. He fell right down onto the footpath, dropping the shopping bags, sending groceries tumbling everywhere and fruit rolling down the gutter.

The checkout lady came squawking out of the supermarket. 'He's fainted...he must have fainted,' I could hear her saying as she scurried around Waxhead like a chicken with its head cut off.

Still hanging onto me, the service station bloke ran across the road to see if he could help. Waxhead looked terrible – his face was as white and dead-looking as paper and his tan had completely faded. He seemed to be out cold.

'Let's carry him inside,' said the service station bloke. And I helped lift Waxhead up and cart his limp body back inside the supermarket. I didn't care about getting caught for stealing any more. All I could think about was whether Waxhead was okay.

But I didn't need to worry. As we lowered him gently down, Waxhead managed to whisper to me, 'Beat it. Meet you back at the Bean.'

A few other people from the shops in the main street had run in to have a sticky-beak. They were all babbling and flapping around, poking at Waxhead, slapping his cheeks, fetching glasses of water. In the middle of all the noise and fuss, no one noticed me slipping down one of the supermarket aisles, through the back storage room and out into the side alley.

I plonked myself down behind a stack of boxes for a moment to catch my breath. I had to admit that Waxhead's fainting act was incredibly impressive. I don't reckon even Rhonda could have done a better job. And if it hadn't been for Waxhead's quick thinking, I would have been a goner. I figured he'd have to keep up the act of being sick for a few minutes and then he'd be able to sneak off and meet me back at the van.

I zig-zagged my way up the alley, ducking behind boxes, just in case Mrs Van der Veen (whose clothes I was wearing, remember) saw me. Peering round the corner in the main street, it took me a couple of seconds to work out what was happening. The supermarket lady and the service station bloke were holding Waxhead's arms and helping him to walk, all wobbly and jelly-legged, back into the street. Waxhead still looked kind of groggy but he was mumbling 'I'm all right, I'm all right' as if he was trying to be very brave about fainting (what a performance!).

So far so good. But then I saw a flash of blue and realised there was a policeman marching down the street towards Waxhead.

'Thank goodness you're here, Sergeant Tortellini,' squawked the supermarket lady. 'This boy fainted and now he seems a bit confused about where his parents are.'

'Ohhh, yes,' said Sergeant Tortellini. 'You don't come from around here, do you, son?'

Waxhead shook his head, in a whoosy sort of way, as if he couldn't think straight.

'Mmm,' groaned the sergeant, looking Waxhead up and down suspiciously through his black-rimmed glasses, with lenses so thick they were like the bottom of a milk bottle. 'I suppose your parents know you're not in school today?'

113

'Ummm...yes...they...excuse me. I'm still feeling...' mumbled Waxhead. (It was champion acting, worth an Academy Award for sure.)

But the cop didn't believe him. He just kept going 'Mmm' with a smirk on his face, as if he reckoned Waxhead was faking it all. I really hate the way adults always reckon kids are lying. I mean, I know in *this* case, Waxhead *was* faking, but the cop didn't know that. Waxhead could have been really crook and, as usual, the adult just assumed the kid must be making it all up to get out of school.

'Can you tell me where your parents are now, son?'

'Umm...well – ' Waxhead began, but before he had to talk his way out of this one, Mrs Van der Veen came tearing across from the service station.

'You took your time getting here, Sergeant!' was the first thing she said. 'That little thief who stole my clothes has disappeared clean away! What are you going to do about finding her and retrieving my property?'

'Well, at the moment,' said Sergeant Tortellini slowly and patiently, as if he was trying not to lose his temper, 'I'm sorting out this young man who seems to have fainted and then –'

'Fainted!' barked Mrs Van der Veen. 'He's probably an accomplice of that little clothes thief!' (Mrs Van der Veen was obviously a smart cookie.)

'Ooh, I don't think so,' said the supermarket lady kindly. 'This boy was just here doing some grocery shopping for his mother.'

'That's right...' mumbled Waxhead groggily, as if he was starting to remember in a hazy sort of way. 'She gave me this list of shopping to do.' And he waved the list I'd written in front of the policeman.

But Mrs Van der Veen was getting impatient. She started waving her arms around wildly, trying to attract the policeman's attention.

'This is all very well, Sergeant, but what about my clothes!'

And with a mighty swipe of her arm, she knocked Sergeant Tortellini's glasses off and into the gutter. The supermarket lady, the service station bloke, Mrs Van der Veen and the sergeant all swooped down to pick up the glasses and collided with each other. Scrambling in the gutter, no one could see what they were doing, until we all heard a definite crunch.

'Oops,' said Mrs Van der Veen. She lifted her foot up slowly to reveal Sergeant Tortellini's glasses in a sad little smashed-up pile.

Sergeant Tortellini squinted up his eyes, trying to focus properly in a bleary-eyed sort of way. He breathed out loudly through his nose in the way people do when they are actually as mad as cut snakes but they don't want to show it. He was obviously trying not to lose his temper. Mrs Van der Veen hopped from foot to foot awkwardly.

She was the kind of person who *hates* admitting that she's wrong. You could see that apologising was actually *painful* for her.

'Well, I suppose I should say – well, Sergeant, I'm – what else can I say but sorry...' was all she could manage to say.

'Accidents happen, Mrs Van der Veen,' he said, with the most fake-looking smile I've ever seen. 'I've got a spare pair somewhere.'

'He's blind as a bat without them,' the super-market lady whispered to the service station bloke.

'And you, young man,' said the sergeant, squinting at Waxhead, 'you can come down to the police station with me while we get in contact with your parents.'

Waxhead didn't have much choice and let himself be led up the street by the half-blind cop. Mrs Van der Veen trotted after them, barking crossly: 'I'd like to make a formal complaint about my stolen clothes, Sergeant. Don't think I'm going to let this matter drop...'

I flopped back among the empty cardboard boxes on the side wall of the supermarket and tried to figure out what to do. The longer I hung around in Wombat Gully, the more risk there was that I'd be caught. But I couldn't do the dirty on Waxhead by leaving him there. I mean, he'd only ended up in this mess because he helped me escape.

After the crummy way I'd treated him, I

wouldn't have blamed Waxhead if he'd run off and left me in Mrs Van der Veen's clutches. I had said I didn't trust anybody. I had said I didn't want to be friends with Waxhead. But when the crunch came, when the chips were down, when I was in Big Trouble, Waxhead had stuck by me.

So I had to stick by him.

CHAPTER 16

IT was all very well deciding that I would help Waxhead escape. But finding a way to do it wasn't so easy.

If Mrs Van der Veen laid her eyes on me, I'd be a goner. If Sergeant Tortellini realised I was the clothes thief, then he'd arrest me and probably Waxhead too. I had no idea what story Waxhead was telling the sergeant at the police station. And anyway, even if I could think up some clever story, there was no way a policeman would let Waxhead go on the word of a kid like me. In general, things looked grim. Impossible.

'What would Rhonda or Barry do in a situation like this?' I asked myself. Neither of them would let an impossible situation stop them. My dad always used to say, 'Gina, if you *think* Impossible, then everything will *be* Impossible. But in fact there are more things in heaven and earth than you can poke a stick at, and if you activate enough brain cells, you'll find a way out of every problem.' (As you can tell, my dad has a pretty unrealistic view of the world, *but* he also has a point.)

Anyway, I came out of the alley and into the main street of Wombat Gully, trying to activate as many brain cells as possible. Next to the supermarket was a hairdresser's shop called Janine's Cut Above Hair and Beauty Salon. In the window were two dummy heads with big curly wigs on them. I've always thought that those huge blond fancy hairdo's look yucky and fake, and while I was thinking this, I suddenly felt my brain cells jumping. I looked from the wigs to Sergeant Tortellini's smashed glasses in the gutter and back to the wigs again.

I had a brainwave. A plan to spring Waxhead from the police station. It was risky, but if I had enough guts, I'd be able to carry it off.

I figured that the only way Sergeant Tortellini would let Waxhead go without a fuss was if his mother came to pick him up. So, I would *be* Waxhead's mother for the afternoon.

Inside Janine's Cut Above Hair and Beauty Salon, there was just one lady having her hair rolled up in curlers. She was busy yakking to the hairdresser and the hairdresser was busy yakking back to her. There was no way I could reach in and swipe one of the wigs out of the window display without them seeing me.

When the hairdresser had finished putting in the curlers, I could hear her offer to make a cup of tea. She lowered a hairdryer over the lady's

119

head and went into the back room. This was the best chance I was likely to get. I had to grab that chance.

Calm and cool as anything, I walked into the salon and picked up a big curly wig.

'Hello,' I said to the lady under the hairdryer, 'I'm just taking this wig so that –'

But the lady pointed to the hairdryer on her head and signalled that she couldn't hear me. So I signalled back to her – flapping my hands in the direction of the hairdresser. I mouthed words at her as if I was explaining why I was taking the wig.

The lady seemed happy to believe me because she smiled and nodded. When I heard the kettle whistle in the backroom, I knew the hairdresser would be back out soon. I quickly made my escape with the stolen wig tucked under my arm.

Next, I peeked into the backyards of quite a few houses to see what was hanging on the clothes-lines. Eventually, I found one with a line full of clothes that looked like they'd belong to a woman about the right age to be Waxhead's mother.

I unpegged a dress made out of flowery material and tried it on over my clothes. The owner of the dress must have been a lot fatter than me, because, even when I added some of the underwear too, the dress still hung on me like a flowery tent. I would need some padding.

A baby was wailing somewhere. I looked over

the fence to where the crying sound came from and saw a clothes-line full of nappies and sheets. Padding!

I peeked through the fence to see a woman on the back verandah. She was pacing up and down, jiggling the crying baby and patting it on the back. If I ducked down behind the sheets, she might not spot me.

Hidden behind a sheet hanging on the line, I started to stuff nappies down inside the underwear. The nappies worked perfectly, making it look as if I filled out the dress.

A gust of wind suddenly whipped the sheet sideways and my cover was gone. I looked up. A pair of eyes looked back at me. The baby was staring straight at me.

I waved and smiled at the baby. The baby pointed back at me and started to burble and screech. I guess it was baby language for 'there's a girl in our garden stuffing nappies down her dress'.

But luckily for me, the mother didn't understand baby language. She just kept on shooshing the baby and jiggling it around. So even though the sharp-eyed baby was pointing straight at the nappy thief (me), I was able to sneak out of the garden safely. All padded out, I looked about the same shape as the lady who owned the dress.

There was one more problem. Shoes. My school shoes didn't suit the disguise but, unfortunately, people don't usually hang their shoes out on the line where kids like me could steal them.

Heading back into town, I was racking my brains for an idea, when I heard a snoring, snuffling sound. On the front porch of a pretty little house, a woman was asleep in a rocking chair, snuffling a bit whenever the chair rocked back. She was wearing exactly the kind of high-heeled shoes I needed. And those shoes were hanging halfway off her feet – as if she'd started to kick them off when she fell asleep.

She didn't wake up as I tiptoed onto the porch and kneeled down beside her. The timing was crucial. If I could catch the moment when she tipped back in the rocking chair, I'd be able to slip the shoes off without her feeling it.

She snuffled, rocked back and I gently slipped off one shoe. I just got my hands on the other shoe, when I heard footsteps behind me.

I turned round slowly. It was the postman, scowling at me. He opened his mouth as if he was about to say something.

'Ssshh...' I whispered, putting a finger to my lips. I pointed at the sleeping woman as if to say 'Don't wake her up'.

The postman winked and nodded. Then he tiptoed away.

Now that I had shoes, I added the final touch of my 'Waxhead's mum' disguise: the big blond curly wig jammed on over the top of my own hair.

It was hard to tell how convincing the disguise

would be. Maybe I just looked like a twelve-year-old kid wearing somebody's mother's clothes. But I had no choice. 'Waxhead's mum' was Waxhead's only chance.

I tottered towards the police station. (Walking in high heels is actually quite hard if you're not used to it.) I was trying to remember what people's mothers sounded like. I needed to practise my mother voice.

As I passed the Wombat Gully Country Women's Association Hall, I felt like someone was following me. I sneaked a sideways look and, sure enough, there was a lady who seemed to be keeping her eye on me. Peering through the blond curls of my wig, I took another look and realised that the woman following me was *me*. Or rather, my reflection in the plate glass windows of the CWA Hall.

It's the weirdest thing – but seeing my reflection all done up in the disguise, I actually started to *feel* like somebody's mother. I didn't feel like Gina Terrific from Year 7 at Muddy Creek High any more. The more I looked, the more I felt as if the fake blond hair, the padded bits and the high heels belonged to me.

Wombat Gully Police Station. As I reached for the door handle, the door swung back in my face and nearly knocked me off my high heels. It was Mrs Van der Veen on her way out. Uh-oh.

I grabbed a handkerchief and pretended to have a sneezing fit into it. If she'd seen my face, it would have been a dead giveaway.

'You're wasting your time in there, lady,' said Mrs Van der Veen crossly to the fat lady in the flowery dress (me). 'That cop is as blind as a bat and as slow as a wet week.'

And without stopping to notice that I was really the clothes thief, Mrs Van der Veen stomped off, muttering crankily to herself.

So Waxhead's mum (me) waltzed straight into the police station and said, 'Good afternoon, Sergeant.'

Sergeant Tortellini was in a real flap. He was rummaging around the station desk and all the drawers, hunting for something. But he was so bleary-eyed without glasses that he kept bumping into things and knocking papers off the desk.

'Oh – um – excuse me a moment, madame,' he said, in a flustered voice. 'If I could just find my spare glasses, I'd be able to – I'll be with you in a moment, madame.'

Through the bubbly glass of a door, I could make out the shape of Waxhead sitting on a chair in the inner office. But unfortunately, there was no way I could signal to him that it was me. I took a deep breath and tried out my mother voice again.

'I believe you've found my son Brian,' I said.

'Oh! Your son, is he?' Sergeant Tortellini looked up, suddenly a lot more interested. He peered at me, squinting up his eyes to try and focus. I hid behind the blond curly wig, almost too scared to breathe in case the policeman saw through the disguise. But Mrs Van der Veen was right – he was as blind as a bat. I suppose when he looked at me all he saw was a fat blur in a pink dress and blond hair.

'He told me his name was Mitch,' said the cop.

'Oh dear, has Brian been telling fibs again, has he?' I said, tut-tutting in the way I thought a mother would.

Sergeant Tortellini tut-tutted too, 'I'm afraid he's caused a lot of people a lot of trouble this afternoon.' Then he called back through the bubbly glass door, 'Brian! Your mother's here to collect you!'

Through the bubbly glass, I saw the shape of Waxhead slump forward on the chair and I heard him moan 'Ohhh no...' (I guess he thought it really was his mother.)

'Out you come, son,' said Sergeant Tortellini sternly. And then he smiled at me in the dear-oh-dear way adults smile about kids. 'Brian has been telling a few unlikely stories. A few tall tales.'

'Brian has quite a vivid imagination,' I explained. 'We've told him time and time again that lying is wrong, but you know what kids are like, Sergeant.'

The bubbly glass door slowly opened and Waxhead stuck his head out sheepishly.

'Hey, that's not –' Waxhead started to say. And then he realised it was me underneath the blond wig and all the padding. Waxhead couldn't stop

himself grinning and I winked to him on the sly.
'Hello, Mum.'

'Don't you "Hello, Mum" me, Brian!' I said,
like a cranky mother. 'What sort of behaviour is
this, mmm? Have you been telling lies to the
sergeant?'

'Sorry, Mum...' mumbled Waxhead, splutt-
ering into giggles.

'I don't think you should be laughing, son,' said
Sergeant Tortellini. 'This is a serious business.'

'That's right, Brian,' I snapped. 'You've put
the sergeant to a lot of trouble.'

'Now, Mrs – uh – what's your surname,
madame?' asked the policeman, squinting at me
blindly.

I didn't have a chance to think and just said the
first name that came into my head. All I could
think of was 'Mitch Maddox', the name of
Waxhead's surfing hero.

'Maddox. Mrs Val Maddox.'

'Well, Mrs Maddox. Brian claims that he was
doing some shopping for you,' said the cop.

'Did you get everything on the list, Brian?' I
said to Waxhead.

'I think so, Mum,' he said.

'Good boy,' I said, starting to enjoy playing
'mother' and bossing Waxhead around. 'Yes, Sergeant, I don't know what lies Brian has told you
but it is true I sent him shopping.'

'Well, then there's the matter of this...uh...
"fainting" business,' said the sergeant
suspiciously.

'Oh no!' I gasped. 'You didn't have another one of your fainting attacks, did you, Brian?'

'I don't know what happened, Mum,' said Waxhead, playing it up for all it was worth, 'one minute I was at the checkout and the next minute everything went black and I was on the ground.'

'You see, Sergeant,' I said, in a Very Serious Parent voice, 'Brian is not a well boy, frankly. We don't know what it is exactly, but the doctors want to do lots of tests. Actually, we're on our way to Sydney right now to the hospital. The sooner we get Brian into hospital the better.'

'I see,' said Sergeant Tortellini, rummaging around for his glasses again. 'What are you doing in Wombat Gully?'

My mind went blank for a minute but Waxhead jumped in with an answer.

'Our car broke down. Dad's getting it fixed.'

'If it's an emergency, I'll drive you to – ' began the policeman.

'Oh no, I'm sure it's fixed by now,' I blabbed out.

'If I could just find these damned spare glasses ...'

'Dad'll be worried, Mum. We'd better go,' said Waxhead, anxious to get out of there.

But I have to admit, I was enjoying myself too much to go straight away. I was enjoying teasing Waxhead, calling him 'Brian' and all that.

'Well, Brian, I hope you've learned your lesson today about telling lies,' I said.

'Yes, Mum.'

'I hope the sergeant has given you a good talking to.'

'Yes, Mum,' said Waxhead, starting to get cross with me.

'Thank you for your help, Sergeant. You've no idea how worried I was about young Brian,' I continued, laying it on a bit thick. 'I apologise for all the trouble Brian has – '

'Let's go, Mum,' said Waxhead through clenched teeth.

Waxhead and I started walking towards the door. Sergeant Tortellini was still frantically searching for his glasses.

'Goodbye, Sergeant,' we both said. And as we got to the door, I really thought we'd made it. But then from behind us, I heard:

'Just a moment.'

We turned round. Sergeant Tortellini had his spare glasses on.

'That's my wife's dress!'

Waxhead and I bolted. We ran as fast as any two kids have ever run, I reckon. But at the first corner, I tripped on the stupid high heels and twisted my ankle. I stopped to pull the shoes off my feet and then had to hobble instead of run. That gave Sergeant Tortellini a chance to catch up with me. Waxhead had run on ahead and I couldn't see him any more. But I heard a shout from across the road.

'Hey!' yelled Waxhead, speeding towards me with a shopping trolley, 'Jump in!'

I jumped into the trolley, on top of our bags of groceries, and Waxhead started to push the trolley down the street at breakneck speed.

'The gas bottle!' I yelled. Waxhead drove the shopping trolley up into the service station and I leaned down to scoop up the caravan's portable gas canister. I hoisted it into the trolley with me and we belted out of the service station.

Sergeant Tortellini was a pretty fast runner and Waxhead was starting to get puffed. The cop was gaining on us. But just past the service station the road suddenly went steeply downhill. Waxhead gave the shopping trolley one more big push and then jumped onto the handle. The trolley hurtled downhill, as fast as a rollercoaster, with Waxhead and me safely onboard.

Up the top of the hill, Sergeant Tortellini groaned and stopped. Red-faced and heaving for breath, he watched us escape.

Down the bottom of the hill, when we knew we were safe, Waxhead and me tumbled off the trolley onto the grass on the riverbank. We were panting, out of breath, and laughing so much we couldn't talk at all.

At that moment, I decided that, whether I liked it or not, Waxhead and me were friends. When you go through an adventure like that with somebody, you just can't help being friends for ever after.

CHAPTER 17

IT wasn't until we'd set sail again in The Baked Bean, that Waxhead let slip his new secret.

'Hey, Girl of Mystery – or should I say, *Gina*,' said Waxhead.

I gasped out loud. How come he knew my name? 'That's not my name,' I lied.

'I'm not as dumb as you think I am, y'know. People always think surfers are dumb, but it's not true.'

'I don't think you're dumb. As a matter of fact, I happen to think you're quite smart,' I said and I meant it too. 'But my name is not Gina or whatever you said.'

Waxhead slapped a piece of paper on the caravan table.

'I found this in the Wombat Gully Police Station,' he said.

It was some kind of leaflet with a lot of writing and a big black headline: MISSING PERSON.

'That's you, isn't it? Right age. Right description. And there can't be too many floating

130

caravans in this part of the country. It's gotta be you,' said Waxhead.

It was me all right. The leaflet had my name in big block letters:

GINA TERRIFIC.

It described exactly what I looked like and how I'd run away from home on the night of the flash flood. The leaflet also mentioned that my caravan had been swept away by the flooded creek.

'Police hold fears for her safety', it said down the bottom. And then: 'Any members of the public with information should contact Constable Brenda Snape of Borrington Police or their nearest police station'.

For a second I felt kind of numb. I flopped back onto the seat like a zombie. Waxhead knew from the look on my face that it was me in the Missing Person leaflet.

'Look, Gina,' he said, sounding a bit sorry that he'd sprung the leaflet on me, 'I know you want to be a Girl of Mystery. So, if you don't want to tell me what happened, I understand.'

'Thanks, Waxhead, I appreciate it,' I said. 'But I reckon I owe you an explanation.'

So, sitting at the little table in The Baked Bean as it scudded downriver towards the sea, I told Waxhead the whole story. All about Barry, Rhonda, Constable Brenda Snape, Dwayne Brickman and the other kids at Muddy Creek High, the Loyalty Oath, and the day I ran away.

I have to admit that I got pretty choked up as

131

I told the story. This was the first time I'd told anyone else about it, remember. But Waxhead was a very good listener. For example, when I started to sniffle and blubber a bit, he just handed me a tissue and didn't make a big deal out of it.

By the time it got dark enough to light the gas lamp, I was up to the part where I met Waxhead at the Hardware Store.

'You know the rest of the story...' I said.

Waxhead didn't say anything for a couple of seconds. He just sat there, soaking it all in, I suppose.

'So – what do you think?' I asked.

'I dunno what to say...' said Waxhead. 'It's a dead sad story, Gina. I mean, to start off with – when you talked about your dad and your friend Rhonda and all that – it sounded beaut. I was kind of jealous. I mean, I'd give anything to have parents like your dad. But then when you got to the part about Rhonda doing the dirty on you with the meathead kids and your dad going all silly over the cop, I reckon I understand how you must've felt. Dead sad. Deadset.'

'So do you reckon I did the right thing? To run away, I mean?' (I wasn't *really* having second thoughts. I just wanted his opinion.)

'Well...are you sure that Rhonda really meant to dump you for those popular kids?'

'Yep,' I said.

'And are you sure your dad meant to dump you for the policewoman?'

'Yep,' I nodded again.

You could tell Waxhead was thinking about it pretty carefully before he made a decision.

'Well then, I guess you didn't have much choice. You had to run away,' Waxhead finally decided.

Waxhead and I stared at the Missing Person leaflet sitting on the caravan table. I have to admit that, for one little minute, I felt kind of proud to have this police leaflet written all about me, with my name in big black letters. I know it sounds childish, but it made me feel sort of important. Big Time.

With the groceries we'd bought in Wombat Gully, we stuffed ourselves full of dinner. I was busy thinking and I could tell Waxhead was too, so neither of us said anything for a long time.

'Do you reckon you'll ever go home, Gina?' asked Waxhead eventually.

'I can't. I vowed I never would. And anyway, what's the point now?' I said. 'No one wants me there anyway. They haven't even tried very hard to look for me, have they?'

'I guess not. So what'll you do?'

'Wander the world. Never stay in one place very long, never have any friends ever again. Stay a loner for ever,' I explained. 'What about you?'

'Haven't really worked it out properly yet,' said Waxheal dreamily. 'I guess I'll travel all over the world being a champion surfer. Hey, maybe I'll run into you once in a while if you're going to be wandering the world too.'

'Maybe,' I said. 'Reckon you'll miss your parents?'

'Well...' said Waxhead thoughtfully, 'my parents aren't like your dad or anything. I mean, they're just your average, ordinary kind of parents. But they're sort of nice. I mean, I like them a lot and everything. But there's no way I can ever go back and live in Possum Hill. No way.'

'Nah,' I agreed. 'No way.'

Lying in bed trying to sleep, I listened to the wind in the trees on the riverbank. I was feeling kind of sick inside – homesick. I don't know for sure about Waxhead, but I reckon he was feeling the same way too. But neither of us said anything about it.

'You awake, Waxhead?' I whispered into the darkness.

'Yeah.'

'I just want to say that I'm really sorry I was so horrible to you before,' I said.

'No worries,' said Waxhead.

'Are you sure you don't mind? I mean, I was pretty nasty to –'

'Nah, don't worry about it. I understand. You had your reasons.'

'You mean you really do forgive me?' I asked.

'Sure,' said Waxhead and even in the dark I could tell he meant it.

'That's very nice of you,' I said.

134

I know I'd made a vow that I'd never have friends or trust anyone ever again. But I decided that I would make an exception in Waxhead's case.

Even when I managed to get to sleep, I dreamed all night about Rhonda eating Mrs Richard's Country Muffins in that TV ad. I dreamed about Barry being at home in Borrington. It made me so homesick I could burst, even in my sleep. Even though I *knew* that no one in Borrington cared about me any more anyway. I guess a person can't control what they dream about.

When the light from the gas lamp shone in my eyes, I thought it was part of my dream at first. Gradually, I realised that I wasn't dreaming and that Waxhead had turned the gas lamp back on. I could see him at the kitchen table, staring at the Missing Person leaflet.

'What's up?' I said sleepily.

'I can't sleep,' he explained. 'I've been thinking about something that cop in Wombat Gully said. He said Constable Brenda Snape was making a big deal about trying to find you. Listen to this bit –'

Waxhead swivelled the leaflet around and, running his grubby fingernail along one of the lines, read it out loud.

'Police have fears for her safety,' he read. 'Hey, do you reckon that means they think maybe you're dead?'

'Oh...I dunno...' I mumbled.

'If you think about it, Gina, your dad and your friend Rhonda don't even know if you're alive or dead. I mean, for all they know, you could've drowned or something.'

'I suppose so...' I admitted. (I hadn't really thought about this before.)

'At least I left my parents a note explaining I'd run away,' said Waxhead. 'I think you should phone up Rhonda and Barry and tell them you're okay.'

'But Tragic Girls of Mystery don't phone home!' I pointed out.

'Well, I reckon it'd be pretty nasty to let your dad think you might be dead. That's my opinion, anyway,' said Waxhead.

Waxhead was right. I had to admit it. Even if Dad and Rhonda didn't care about me any more, they ought to be told I was still alive. I'd been so busy running away and being a Tragic Girl of Mystery that I'd never even stopped to think about stuff like that. To tell the truth, I felt pretty mean about it.

I knew I'd never get back to sleep that night unless I managed to send a message to Dad and Rhonda that I was okay. So, even though it was pitch dark on the river, I had to get to a telephone.

CHAPTER 18

ACCORDING to the map, there was a tiny railway station on the south side of the river a little way downstream. I figured that was my best chance of finding a telephone. So we anchored The Baked Bean under the railway bridge which ran across the river.

'You don't have to come with me, you know,' I said to Waxhead as I climbed out through the caravan roof hatch.

Waxhead shrugged. 'Do you want me to come with you?'

Tragic Girls of Mystery are not *supposed* to need friends. They are not supposed to need anyone. But I didn't feel like being alone that night. So I said, really cool, as if I didn't care all that much, 'If you feel like it.'

Waxhead and I waded ashore and started following the train tracks inland. Even in the pitch blackness of the bush, the steel ribbon of the rail tracks glinted bright and clear.

A wild wind had sprung up and whooshed along

the rail-line like an invisible train going past. Some gusts of wind were so strong, it was hard to keep our balance on the tracks.

I couldn't help thinking about all the times Rhonda and me had spent hanging around the train tracks outside Borrington. We used to balance along the railway line like tightrope walkers, talking our heads off for hours without getting bored. 'But,' I thought, 'I'll never do that with Rhonda ever again.' I wondered if Rhonda was balancing along the train tracks with one of her new Muddy Creek High friends.

I guess the dawn was starting to break because we could see the sky getting lighter. But it was so cloudy, there was no pretty sunrise. The sky was a miserable grey colour.

Eventually, we saw the little wooden shed of the train station up ahead. And, sure enough, beside the station hut was a public telephone. The fluorescent light inside the phone-box was the only light you could see anywhere. It made the phone-box look kind of weird and spooky, standing all alone and bright in the middle of nowhere.

Facing the telephone, with the coins ready in my hand to make the call, I lost my nerve. I chickened out. I just couldn't do it.

'Give me those,' said Waxhead, grabbing the coins out of my hand. 'I'll phone up for you. Just tell me the number.'

'Thanks, Waxhead,' I said.

Waxhead dialled the number of the house

where my dad lived (and where I *used* to live) and I listened though the glass door of the phone booth.

As soon as the phone was answered, Waxhead had his speech ready. 'Hello. You don't know me,' he said. 'I have a message from Gina Terrific. She told me to tell you that she is okay and she has run away for ever.'

The plan was that Waxhead would hang up the phone after he'd said the message. But he didn't hang up. He seemed to be listening to someone talking on the other end of the line. I signalled through the glass 'Hang up!' but he was too busy listening.

I heard him say, 'Oh...umm...I can't say...I promised –'

Then he listened again for what seemed like ages. I was jumping up and down outside the phone-box. I wanted to know what was going on. I wanted Waxhead to hang up the stupid phone.

The wind was whipping up even stronger, making a whooshing noise around the little railway station. It was starting to rain too, big fat plops of rain landing on my hair. With the noise of the wind, I could only just hear a few words Waxhead was saying. Stuff like 'How did you know that?' and 'Umm...no, I'd better not say anything...' Why didn't he hang up? Who was he talking to?

I was about to barge into the phone-box and pull him away from the phone when a diesel train

139

roared past, pulling about twenty carriages loaded with sheep. The tiny station hut and the phone-box shook with the vibration of the train, and the noise was deafening. Waxhead was trying to hear something on the other end of the phone line, but with the train trundling past, it was no use. He hung up.

When Waxhead came out of the phone-box, he looked like a stunned mullet. He mumbled something about 'Amazing...'

'You were meant to hang up straight after the message!' I said crossly. 'Who were you talking to all that time? My dad?'

'No. Your friend Rhonda,' said Waxhead.

'Ha!' I said. 'That traitor! I don't want to know about it!'

'But, Gina, she said –'

'It's starting to rain. If we don't get back to the caravan fast we'll get soaking wet,' I said, flouncing off in the direction of the river.

Waxhead scurried after me, trying to get me to listen.

'Gina, wait! It was amazing!' he said. 'Rhonda figured out who I was! She worked out that we're travelling together! She also said something about a guy at a petrol station finding a piece of your school uniform and that's how she –'

'I said I don't want to hear about anything that person said,' I snapped, stomping off down the railway tracks. My feet kept skidding because the rain was making the tracks slippery.

'But, Gina, you thought no one in Borrington cared about you any more. But it's not true! Rhonda said Constable Snape's been up all day and night organising search parties and everything! You said Constable Snape didn't want you around, but she's got the whole police force looking for you!'

I tried to block my ears with my hands. I didn't want to hear any of this. The rain was really bucketing down now, and the wind was thwacking my wet hair into my eyes like a whip. In the air all around us, we could feel the electric charge of another huge storm building. But Waxhead didn't let up. He followed close behind me, shouting above the noise of the wind and rain.

'Rhonda asked me to give you a message too,' he said. 'She said to tell you that breaking the Loyalty Oath was the most disgusting thing she's ever done and she probably doesn't deserve to be forgiven. But because being best friends with you is the most important thing in the world, she hopes you'll accept her apology.'

'Ha!' I snorted.

'Gina!' yelled Waxhead, confused about why I was being so stubborn. 'You should have heard how sorry she was! You should have heard how worried they all are about you!'

From the outside, I tried to look as if I didn't care. I just kept stomping along the rail tracks back to the river. But inside, I was incredibly choked up. Too choked up to speak, in fact.

'Far out, Gina. I reckon you're so lucky to have a friend like Rhonda...I mean, you have to forgive her. You have to make up with Rhonda now.'

'I can't,' I said.

'Eh?'

'I can't forgive Rhonda even if I want to,' I said. 'I made a vow that I'd never forgive her and a person should never break a vow.'

'But that's just stupid,' said Waxhead, starting to lose his temper with me. 'You can't let some stupid vow mess things up! What's the point of making vows if it just makes everybody feel crummy? That's really dumb if you ask me. I reckon it's dumb and *mean*.'

'I wasn't the one who was mean. Rhonda was the one who –' I started to explain.

'Aww, who are you kidding, Gina? You can't hold things against people for ever. I mean everybody says stuff they don't mean sometimes. You don't deserve to have good friends if you just act sulky and stubborn and mean to them.' Waxhead was really letting me have it.

'But I made the vow because –'

'Why don't you think about other people instead of just thinking about your dumb vow? Fair dinkum, Gina, I don't reckon I've ever met anyone as stubborn as you. You must be the most stubborn person in the entire world!'

Maybe Waxhead was right. But at that moment, I didn't know what to think. Up till then,

I had everything worked out in my head. But now – running through the pouring rain with Waxhead yelling at me above the noise of the storm – everything seemed upside down all of a sudden.

'Who asked your opinion anyway? It's none of your business!' I bellowed at Waxhead.

I felt so mad with Waxhead, I could have thumped him. Sometimes, when a person is telling you something you don't want to hear, when a person is making you realise your mistakes, you hate their guts. Sometimes, you can dig your heels in so far and you get stuck.

I needed to talk stuff over with someone. Rhonda was usually the person I could talk about a problem with. Maybe if Waxhead stopped shouting at me for a second, I could talk to him.

But before I had a chance to say anything, I heard Waxhead scream out 'Oh no!' When I turned round to look down at the river, I saw what he was hollering about.

We'd left The Baked Bean tied up to the railway bridge, but now that the storm had hit, the poor old Bean was being battered and smashed around by gusts of wind and swirling floodwater.

Heavy rain was pelting down, drenching everything and raising the level of the river minute by minute. The sky was weighed down with layers of soggy black clouds, ready for more downpours. Wind was buffeting round and round us as if we were trapped in a huge tumble drier. Instead of our quiet peaceful river there was now a mass of

143

brown swirling water churning its way through the valley like a gigantic bulldozer.

It wouldn't be long before the rope gave way and the Bean was snatched away by the flooded river. But there was no safe way to get to the caravan. It didn't look like there was any chance of saving it.

'My board!' wailed Waxhead. We could just see the red fin of Waxhead's surfboard sticking up out of the boiling water. The rope holding the surfboard to the caravan was frayed and it was only a matter of minutes before the board would be torn loose and be lost for ever. Without stopping to use his brain, Waxhead scrambled down the muddy slope towards the river.

'I'm gonna get my board back,' he said.

'Don't be crazy!' I yelled, tugging at his arm to pull him back from the river's edge. 'The current's too strong! You won't be able to swim through that!'

But Waxhead wasn't really listening. All he could think about was his surfboard.

'You don't understand, Gina. I've gotta get my board.'

'It's just a dumb surfboard, Waxhead! Don't be crazy! Don't –'

But it was too late. He was diving in. I lunged across to stop him. But as Waxhead threw himself forward into the river, I lost my footing on the muddy bank and tumbled headfirst into the churning water of the Bodgee Bodgee River.

CHAPTER 19

WAXHEAD was an incredibly good swimmer (on account of being a surfer and all that), but the pull of the roaring floodwater was so strong that even he was struggling. So I didn't have a chance.

I pounded my arms and legs through the water, but however hard I swam, the river just picked me up and threw me around like a bit of old junk.

Waxhead seemed to disappear into the river and then all I could see was churning brown water. The river tumbled me over and over like a dumper wave at the beach. I spluttered and gasped, swallowing gulps of water as I tried to work out which way was up.

When I started gulping air instead of water, I knew my head must have bobbed to the surface. It was useless trying to swim against the pull of the river, so I let myself be swept along.

Rain started pouring down so heavily it splashed up off the surface of the water. It made a kind of haze across the river, a fine spray all round me so I couldn't see where I was going. The roar of the floodwater filled my ears. Somewhere I thought I heard someone calling out my name

For a second, I wondered if I'd died. Maybe this is what it felt like to die, I thought. And at that moment, I knew for sure that Waxhead was right.

I had been stubborn and sulky and incredibly stupid. I thought about Rhonda trying so hard to find me. I thought about my dad getting so upset and worried about me. I would've burst into tears right there in the middle of the Bodgee Bodgee except I was too out of breath to cry. I didn't deserve to have a friend like Rhonda and a father like Barry. Waxhead had tried to talk some sense into me but I wouldn't listen. Waxhead had been a good friend to me and now he was probably drowned. I'd acted like a stupid little kid. I'd had a little kid's tantrum. Childish and thoughtless and absolutely pathetic.

I felt something hard bump against me. It was a forty-four gallon drum, scudding along the top of the water. I grabbed onto the steel drum and flopped my arms over it. Hanging onto the drum, I could at least keep my head above the water. I gulped for air like a gasping fish stranded on the beach. The rain pounded on my back like a shower on full blast and strong gusts of wind whipped and flapped my wet clothes around me. I felt freezing cold right through to my bones.

I heard a voice calling 'Gina! Gina!' Then I realised it was Waxhead's voice calling my name. Through the haze of rain, I could see him reaching out a hand to me.

Somehow, Waxhead had managed to swim to The Baked Bean just before it tore loose from its mooring. The caravan was now being swept downriver, alongside the forty-four gallon drum. Waxhead was holding onto the van's tow-bar with one hand, reaching out to save me with his other hand. It wasn't until I heard him speak that I was sure I was really still alive.

'C'mon, Gina. Grab my hand! You can do it!' he yelled.

Waxhead grabbed my arm and, pulling hard against the drag of the river, he hauled me up to where I could latch on to the tow-bar with one hand. Just then I noticed a red fin sticking out.

'Your board!' I yelled. Waxhead's surfboard was wedged against one of the mudguards of the caravan. I saw Waxhead's face light up with joy when he spotted it. I knew how much his board meant to him.

'I'll see if I can –' I panted, reaching for the board.

'Don't worry about it. Too dangerous,' Waxhead shouted. 'Climb up quick! It's just a dumb surfboard! Quick, before the –'

'I've got it!' I shouted triumphantly.

I got my other hand around the surfboard fin. Waxhead pulled me and the surfboard up onto the tow-bar and we hoisted the board and ourselves in through the roof hatch.

'I'm sorry, Gina. I'm sorry I got us into this mess,' said Waxhead.

The roar of the river and the wind was so loud we had to shout like crazy to hear each other.

'Don't worry about it, Waxhead,' I said.

Rain pelted onto the roof and the wind hissed and howled around the van windows. The storm seemed to be whipping itself up into a huge tantrum aimed straight at us.

Sopping wet and shivering cold and scared out of our wits, we pulled blankets round ourselves and turned the gas stove on full blast to warm ourselves up. At least we felt a whole lot better once we were back inside The Baked Bean. Mind you, we weren't *really* much safer. But the van was home, so we *felt* safer.

Scudding along in the water was an incredible amount of junk. Furniture, boxes, trees, bits of cars, part of a wooden bridge and lots of stuff that you couldn't recognise any more. The greedy river seemed to be sucking *everything* downstream with it.

And to be honest, the mighty Baked Bean was really just one more bit of junk caught up in the churning water. I mean, we'd be kidding ourselves if we thought we were 'sailing' the Bean any more. We didn't have any choice about where we were going. The caravan was being scooped along by the floodwater whether we liked it or not. Completely out of control.

148

'What do you reckon we should do now?' I asked.

'Well there's no way we can swim ashore through that,' said Waxhead. 'But I'm not sure how much longer the Bean is going to hold up.'

The Baked Bean was lurching around, colliding with the other flotsam and jetsam, spinning and tipping in the strong current. A couple of times, I really thought it would tip right over and Waxhead and me would be goners. At any moment, the churning river might smash the little caravan (with us inside) against something – just like smashing a tiny matchbox.

For a while, Waxhead and I didn't say much to each other. I'm not saying we weren't dead scared. Frankly, we were. But the thing is, at a time like that, your brain is working overtime to think of a way out. You don't waste time yakking. We just sat silently, watching the water drip off the surfboard onto the floor. I wondered what Waxhead was thinking about, and to tell the truth, I was busting to tell him what I was thinking.

'Waxhead,' I said, kind of nervously, 'if I say something, will you promise not to laugh?'

'Sure,' he said, 'if you promise not to laugh when I say something.'

'Okay. We'll say what we want to say at exactly the same time. One, two three –'

And then we both said exactly the same thing. This is absolutely true. In unison, we said, 'I want to go home.'

And both spluttered into uncontrollable giggles. When we recovered from our laughing fit, we realised that we were still in Big Trouble. Deciding to go home hadn't really solved any of our problems at that particular moment.

'Do you reckon we're going to die?' I asked.

'Nah,' said Waxhead, but he didn't sound all that sure.

'Well, if I die and you don't die,' I said, 'will you tell Rhonda and Dad I'm really sorry and I forgive them and I apologise for causing all this trouble?'

'Sure. If you'll promise to tell my parents I'm sorry and that I really like them and all that. That's if I die and you don't die,' said Waxhead.

'It's a deal,' I said and we shook hands to seal the deal.

'But if we both die...' mumbled Waxhead.

'Then they'll never know we were sorry. They'll never know we really wanted to go home,' I pointed out.

Waxhead nodded and we sank into a gloomy silence.

'But we're not going to die,' said Waxhead pulling himself together. 'There's got to be a way out of this mess.'

'You're right,' I said, pulling myself together too. 'Let's think about this logically.'

'The map!' said Waxhead, jumping up to find it. 'That might give us an idea.'

We spread the map out on the table and

worked out where we were. We peered at the map, hoping to find a bridge or an island or something – *anything* that might help us get ashore and get home. It was the same crummy map I'd bought at the grotty service station, covered in black greasy splodges and smears.

'What's that? Under that grease blob?' asked Waxhead.

'I dunno...it says "Murrumbodgee..." something – I can't read the second word,' I said. 'It might be something useful though. It might be ...'

Waxhead stuck his head out the window to have a good look. I spat on my finger and scrubbed at the black spot hoping to read what was underneath.

'Uh-oh, Gina,' groaned Waxhead in a Voice of Doom. 'I think I know what the second word is.'

'It says "Murrumbodgee...Dam!"' I screeched.

'Look!' said Waxhead, pointing out the window.

Through the pelting rain and fog, we could see huge red signs along the riverbank:

WARNING: MURRUMBODGEE DAM UNSTABLE DUE TO FLOOD DAMAGE

And then a bit further along, another sign:

DANGER. DAM WALL COLLAPSED. DANGER.

We'd been in Big Trouble before. But now we were in the BIGGEST TROUBLE I'd ever been in, in my whole life.

CHAPTER 20

WE tried everything we could think of. We tried throwing out the anchor to slow ourselves down. We tried hooking ropes around trees to stop the van. When we had no ropes left and nothing else to use as an anchor, we were still in Big Trouble. We were still hurtling, out of control, towards the collapsed Murrumbodgee Dam.

'I guess we'll just have to try and swim to the bank,' I suggested, trying not to sound too hopeless.

'I wonder how close we are,' said Waxhead and he pulled himself up through the roof hatch to take a look. 'Hey, come and check this out, Gina!'

'I don't wanna look!' I shouted back. I couldn't bear to look. To see the riverbank – to see how close we were to being safe and going home – just made me feel crummier.

'A car! It's a – it's a police car I reckon!' yelled Waxhead.

I scrambled up through the roof hatch and we

both strained to see across to the bank. A police car was zooming up the road that ran alongside the river.

'Someone's waving!' said Waxhead.

'That's my dad!' I gasped.

Driving the police car and waving across to us, was Barry. And then I realised that in the seat beside him was Rhonda!

'What's that behind them?' I asked. 'A truck ...Val and Brian's Hardware –'

'My parents!' said Waxhead, waving to them like a maniac.

The police car and the hardware truck sped along the riverbank abreast with the caravan. Then Rhonda leaned right out the window of the car and yelled across the river in a booming voice, 'I'm sorry, Gina!'

'No, *I'm* the one who's sorry!' I yelled back.

Rhonda said some more stuff about how badly she'd acted and how much she missed me and all that. Some of the words got blown away or drowned out by the storm, but I got the message loud and clear.

'Can we be best friends again, please?' I bellowed to her.

'You bet!' shouted Rhonda with a huge grin that anyone could have seen from ten kilometres away.

'I'm sorry too!' Barry yelled across.

And while Dad and me were busy apologising to each other across the flooded river, Waxhead and his parents did the same. Everyone was so busy saying sorry and all that stuff, that for a moment, we forgot about the danger.

Now we were close enough to the collapsed dam to *see* how incredibly dangerous it was up ahead. Through the haze, we could see where the level of the river suddenly dropped down, where the dam wall used to be. The water swirled round and cascaded down, sucking all the junk down with it.

I pointed up ahead, yelling out about the collapsed dam, trying to make Dad understand we needed help. He just yelled back 'Don't worry!' a few times.

It was all very well for Barry to say 'Don't worry', but we were careering straight towards the huge drop with no way of stopping ourselves. What was the point of everyone making up with each other if we were smashed up at the bottom of the dam?

'Who's *that*?' Waxhead gasped.

And then I realised why Dad had told me not to worry. On a rocky outcrop on the other bank of the river, an amazing sight appeared. A lone figure on horseback.

'That's Constable Brenda Snape and Zorro,' I explained to Waxhead.

Brenda Snape was in her fabulous rodeo star outfit – sparkly white with red tassels. A lightning strike cracked across the sky and flashed against the spangles on Brenda's hat and on Zorro's bridle like a laser beam. Brenda was twirling a lassoo above her head.

Suddenly, along both sides of the river, more rodeo riders appeared. Brenda's mates. About half a dozen of them. They were all rodeo champions, galloping their horses along the banks to keep level with the caravan.

As The Baked Bean was sucked closer and closer to the edge, Brenda and the rodeo riders threw their lassoo ropes out across the water. They had fantastic aim. Two of the ropes missed and dropped into the river but the others hooked onto the caravan somewhere. A couple of lassoos looped themselves onto the windows, one onto the tow-bar, and the rest hooked onto the brackets where the awning used to be attached.

Half a second before the Bean would have plummeted over the dam, the rodeo riders' lassoos yanked it back. The riders wound their ropes around trees on the bank. As the van lurched in the water, the ropes snapped tight, but the strength of the tree trunks held firm. For the moment at least. I heard a cheer from the bank and looked up through the roof hatch to see Dad and Rhonda and everybody whooping with joy. Waxhead and me waved and cheered back.

Brenda and the rodeo champions had saved the day – or so we all thought for a second or two. But then we realised the danger was not over. The Bean was not safe from the swirling flood-waters. The river and the wind between them were buffeting the van against the jagged hunks of the broken dam wall. The van was creaking and groaning as if it might break apart any moment. Apart from that, the lassoo ropes couldn't possibly hold the van for more than a few seconds longer.

Then there was a mighty bump that jarred the whole van. I felt it in my guts like a sickening thump. A piece of the broken concrete had smashed through the van's waterproof hull. Water was gushing into the van through the hole like a tap turned on full blast.

We had to get out of that caravan and onto dry land. Fast. I could see the panic on the faces of our friends on the shore. But there didn't seem to be anything they could do to save us. It looked like the van would smash into tiny pieces and take us with it, over the edge.

Then I had a brainwave. It wasn't such a fabulous brainwave really. But it was probably the Most Important Brainwave of my whole life.

'Waxhead!' I blurted out. 'Your board!'

I shoved the surfboard up through the roof hatch so that Brenda could see it. From the far riverbank, I saw Brenda Snape give me a 'thumbs up' signal.

Waxhead and I eased the board down towards the water. Then Brenda twirled another lassoo rope above her white sparkly hat. With mind-boggling aim, she managed to lassoo the tail fin of the surfboard.

Waxhead launched the surfboard into the water and kneeled on it. I kneeled behind him, hanging on like a motorbike pillion rider. Brenda started to wind in the rope. The river was churning and swirling underneath us, but Waxhead had fabulous balance (because of surfing) and he managed to keep us upright.

Slowly, slowly, Brenda pulled us ashore, until we collapsed onto the riverbank, flopping ourselves out on solid ground at last.

I felt like I'd just been through the wash-and-spin cycle of a washing machine. I looked up to see Brenda the Rodeo Star grinning down at me.

'Thanks a lot, Brenda,' I said and I'd never felt so grateful to anyone in my life.

'Don't mention it, Gina,' she said, in her laid-back way. 'No worries.'

I got to my feet and waved across to Dad and Rhonda on the other side to show them I was all right. I turned back just in time to see The Baked Bean sucked over the edge of the broken dam. It crashed onto the piles of concrete and rubbish below, battered and bashed like an old shoebox. Broken pieces of caravan and bits I recognised from Barry's inventions were being sucked away downriver.

I got pretty choked up to see the mighty Bean smashed up like that. I grew up in that caravan – lived in it my whole life until Borrington. I knew every inch of that van and now all the gadgets and fittings and doodads that I loved were broken and swept away.

But as Dad and me decided later on, you can't sulk and brood about losing things like that. It was sad to see the Bean go, that was for sure. But Barry and me agreed that it was a pretty good ending for The Baked Bean – burial at sea for a noble van.

On the way home, Rhonda and Barry filled me in on what had happened at their end of things. It turned out that Dad had been so upset about me running away, that he'd gone completely to pieces. But Rhonda and Brenda had joined forces and put their brains together to track me down.

The first clue was the piece of school uniform I'd torn off near Boris Crump's house. Then there was the I.O.U. note I left at Waxhead's hardware store and Sergeant Tortellini's story about our adventure at Wombat Gully. The final hint, that helped Brenda and Rhonda pinpoint where we were, was Waxhead's phonecall. Rhonda heard the goods train roaring past in the background, so Brenda checked the train timetables, and worked out there was only one place it could be. I told Brenda she should be a detective, but she just laughed and shrugged her shoulders.

Anyway, running away and travelling down the river seems like *ages* ago, now that things are back to normal (sort of) in Borrington. But I guess you might want to know how things ended up afterwards.

One of the first things I did when I got home was to write apology letters to all the people I'd stolen things from and stuff like that. To Boris Crump, Mrs Van der Veen, Sergeant Tortellini. Janice's Cut Above Hair and Beauty Salon, and so on. I posted back the clothes I'd borrowed and paid back any money I owed. I still felt pretty lousy about stealing, but apologising was better than doing nothing.

Things worked out beaut for Waxhead. My dad got talking to Mr and Mrs McKellen (Waxhead's parents) and told them The Barry Terrific Theory About Parents and Kids. He told them it was his opinion that kids should have equal, or almost equal, vote in what a family decides to do. Mr and Mrs McKellen could see Dad's point and they decided that, since it meant *so* much to Waxhead, they would move back to the coast.

The McKellens sold the hardware store at Possum Hill and started a cafe on the beach called The Surfer's Paradise which is incredibly popular now. Waxhead ended up back with all his surfing mates and I got a postcard last week to say he was through to the finals of the Junior Australian Surfing Championship.

Yep, Waxhead and me are still friends, even though we live a long way apart. We write each other letters, and next summer, Rhonda and me are going to have two weeks holiday at his place.

Waxhead is going to teach us to surf. I really want Waxhead and Rhonda to get to know each other because I reckon they'd get on like a house on fire.

Brenda and me are friends too. I never really understood Brenda before because she's so different to Dad and me. I mean, she isn't a motor-mouth for a start. But you just have to learn to *understand* someone like Brenda Snape and then everything's cool. Brenda is teaching me to ride Zorro which is unreal fun.

Barry and Brenda are going to get married at next year's Burragoranga Rodeo and I'm really happy about it. Sometimes I get a teensy weensy bit jealous when Dad and Brenda go all lovey-dovey together. I'd be fibbing if I didn't admit that. But Dad and me have a new policy of making time to mooch around together, working on inventions or whatever – just the two of us. So it's actually good value having Brenda around too.

When I first got home, Rhonda and me raved on and on about how disgusting we'd been to each other, apologising and bad-mouthing ourselves like crazy. It actually started to get sort of boring.

So we agreed that we wouldn't mention it for a while and would just get on with being best friends. In fact, I reckon our friendship is even *stronger* now that it's been tested like that.

Muddy Creek High isn't so bad these days.

Because I was in all the newspapers and the story got round school about what happened to me, the other kids were all terribly impressed. I guess they thought it was glamorous to run away, to get swept away in a flood and be rescued and all that. I suppose you could say I'm pretty popular at Muddy Creek High now, but there's no way I'm going to let it go to my head. For example, I still happen to think Dwayne Brickman is a meathead.

When I think about all my plans to be a Tragic Girl of Mystery and wander the world all alone, I get pretty embarrassed. I mean, I had some incredibly childish, unrealistic, dumb ideas. But that doesn't mean I've given up on the idea of wandering the world and going to places like Bagdad and Rio di Janeiro and Siberia. Actually, you could say I've got the itch to travel.

I'd like to have a go at proper sailing – you know, with an actual boat and sails and all that. Over sausages and mash the other night, I mentioned to Dad – just making conversation – that it might be fun if the whole Terrific family (Dad, Brenda and me) sailed around the world.

'That's a beaut idea, Gina!' said Barry, gulping down a mouthful of sausage and mash. And you know what Dad's like once he gets an idea into his head...

About the author

Debra Oswald began writing in her teens and now works as a scriptwriter in film, television, radio and the theatre. Her credits include the ABC TV series 'Palace of Dreams' and 'Sweet and Sour'. Debra's stage play *Dags*, a comedy of teenage angst, has been performed around Australia, New Zealand and Britain and is published by Currency Press.

Debra's first novel about Gina and Barry – *Me and Barry Terrific* – is published by Oxford University Press and has recently been translated into French.

Debra lives in Sydney and enjoys movies, food, yakking to her friends, building a house in the bush and playing with her three-year-old son.